A NOTE ON THE AUTHOR

JUDITH SCHALANSKY was born in 1980 in Greifswald in the former East Germany. She studied art history and communication design and works as a freelance writer in Berlin. Schalansky's previous book *Atlas of Remote Islands* won the Stiftung Buchkunst (Book Art Foundation) award for 'the most beautiful book of the year' and was published to acclaim in the UK and the USA in 2010. *The Giraffe's Neck* is her first novel to be published in English. She lives in Berlin.

A NOTE ON THE TRANSLATOR

SHAUN WHITESIDE is a translator from German, French, Italian and Dutch. His translations from German include novels by Bernhard Schlink, Pascal Mercier, Zoran Drvenkar and Marlen Haushofer, as well as works by Freud, Nietzsche, Musil and Schnitzler. His translation of Lilian Faschinger's *Magdalena the Sinner* won the 1996 Schlegel-Tieck Translation Prize. He lives in London with his wife and son.

Judith Schalansky
The Giraffe's Neck

TRANSLATED FROM THE GERMAN BY SHAUN WHITESIDE

B L O O M S B U R Y

LONDON · NEW DELHI · NEW YORK · SYDNEY

Originally published in Germany in 2011 under the title
Der Hals der Giraffe by Suhrkamp Verlag

First published in Great Britain 2014
Copyright © 2011 by Suhrkamp Verlag Berlin
English translation copyright © 2014 by Shaun Whiteside
This paperback edition published 2015

The moral right of the author has been asserted

Illustration on p 10 reproduced with permission of BLV Buchverlag
Barbara von Damnitz copyright © BLV Buchverlag
Illustration on pp 20–21 reproduced with permission of DK Images
Peter Visscher copyright © Dorling Kindersley

The translation of this work was supported by a grant from the Goethe-
Institut, which is funded by the German Ministry of Foreign Affairs

Bloomsbury Publishing plc
50 Bedford Square
London
WC1B 3DP

www.bloomsbury.com

Bloomsbury Publishing, London, New Delhi, New York and Sydney

Bloomsbury is a trademark of Bloomsbury Publishing Plc

A CIP catalogue record for this book is available from the British Library

ISBN 978 1 4088 3779 5
10 9 8 7 6 5 4 3 2 1

Typeset by Hewer Text UK Ltd, Edinburgh
Printed and bound in Great Britain by CPI Group (UK) Ltd, Croydon CR0 4YY

Contents

Ecosystems   1

Genetic Processes   75

Evolution Theory   165

Ecosystems

'Sit down,' said Inge Lohmark, and the class sat down. She said, 'Open the book at page one,' and they opened the book at page one, and then they started on ecological balances, ecosystems, the interdependencies and inter-relations between species, between living creatures and their environment, the effective organisation of commu-nity and space. From the food web of mixed woodland they moved to the food chain of the field, from the rivers to the seas and finally to the desert and the tidal flats. 'You see, no one – no animal, no human being – can live entirely for himself alone. Competition prevails between living creatures. And sometimes, too, something like cooper-ation. But that is rather rare. The most significant forms of coexistence are competition and the relationship between predator and prey.'

While Inge Lohmark drew arrows on the board, from the mosses, lichens and fungi to the earthworms and stag beetles, hedgehogs and shrews, then to the great tit, to the roe deer and the hawk, and finally one last arrow to the wolf, a pyramid gradually formed, with man at its tip along-side a few beasts of prey.

'The fact is that there is no animal that eats eagles or lions.'

She took a step back to consider the big chalk drawing.

The arrow diagram linked producers with primary, secondary and tertiary consumers as well as the inevitable decomposing micro-organisms, all connected by respiration, heat loss and increase in biomass. In nature everything had its place, and if perhaps not every creature had a purpose, then at least every species did: eating and being eaten. It was wonderful.

'Copy that down in your exercise books.'

As she said, so it was done.

This was when the year began. The unease of June was long past, the time of sultry heat and bare upper arms. The sun glared through the glass façade, turning the classroom into a greenhouse. The expectation of summer germinated somewhere in the back of empty minds. The mere prospect of wasting their days in utter futility robbed the children of all their concentration. With swimming-pool eyes, greasy skin and a sweaty urge for freedom they slumped on their chairs and dozed their way towards the holidays. Some became erratic and insane. Others, because of the coming report, feigned submissiveness and deposited their biology assessments on the teacher's desk like cats laying dead mice on the sitting-room carpet. Only to ask, at the next class, for their marks, calculators at the ready, eager to work out the improvement in their average to three decimal points.

But Inge Lohmark wasn't one of those teachers who caved in at the end of the school year just because they were about to lose their adversaries. She wasn't worried about slipping into insignificance as she was thrown back entirely on her own devices. Some of her colleagues, the closer the summer break approached, were afflicted with almost tender pliancy. Their teaching degenerated into a hollow form of audience participation. A dreamy glance here, a pat on the back there, wistful encouragement, hours of miserable film-watching. An inflation of good marks, a grievous betrayal of the A-grade. And then there was the nuisance of rounding up end-of-year marks to heave a few hopeless cases up into the next class. As if that helped anybody at all. Her colleagues simply didn't understand that they were just damaging their own health by showing any interest in their pupils. After all, they were nothing but bloodsuckers who drained you of all your vital energy. Who fed on the teaching body, on its authority and its fear, doing harm to its responsibility. They constantly ambushed one. With nonsensical questions, meagre suggestions and distasteful familiarities. The purest vampirism.

Inge Lohmark wasn't going to be sucked dry any more. She was well known for her ability to maintain a tight rein and a short leash, without flying into rages or throwing bunches of keys. And she was proud of it. One could still show weakness. The occasional carrot, out of nowhere.

The important thing was to set the pupils in the right direction, put blinkers on them in order to sharpen their concentration. And if chaos really did prevail, you just had to scrape your fingernails down the board or tell them about the canine tapeworm. In any case the best thing was to make the pupils constantly aware that they were at her mercy. Rather than allowing them to think they had anything to say. Her pupils had no right to speak and no opportunity to choose. No one had a choice. There were natural breeding choices and that was that.

The year started now. Even though it had begun a long time ago. For her it started today, on the first of September, which fell on a Monday this year. And it was now, in the dried-up tail-end of summer, that Inge Lohmark made her resolutions, not on gaudy New Year's Eve. She was always glad that her school planner carried her safely over the turn of the calendar year. A simple flick of the page, with no countdown or clinking of glasses.

Inge Lohmark looked across the three rows of desks and didn't move her head so much as an inch. She had perfected it down the years: the omnipotent, motionless gaze. According to statistics, there were always at least two in the class who were really interested in the subject. But those statistics seemed to be in jeopardy. Regardless of the rules of Gaussian distribution. How on earth had they managed to get this far? You could tell they'd been doing nothing but loaf around for six weeks. None of them had opened a single book. The big holidays. Not quite as big as they used to be. But still far too long! It would take at least a month to get them used to the school's biorhythm again. At least she didn't have to listen to their stories. They could tell those to Mrs Schwanneke, who organised an icebreaking game with each new class. After half an hour all the participants were entangled in skeins from a red ball of wool, and could each rattle off the names and hobbies of the child sitting next to them.

Just a few scattered seats were occupied. It was clear

now how few they were. A sparse audience in her theatre of nature: twelve pupils – five boys, seven girls. The thirteenth had gone back to technical school, even though Mrs Schwanneke had intervened forcefully on his behalf. With repeated private lessons, home visits and psychological reports. Some sort of concentration problem. The things they came up with! These developmental problems they'd read about somewhere or other. First there was dyslexia, then dyscalculia. What next? An allergy to biology? Back in the old days there were just pupils who were bad at sport or music. And they had to play and sing along with everyone else anyway. It was merely a matter of willpower.

It just wasn't worth it, dragging the weak ones along with you. They were nothing but millstones that held the rest back. Born recidivists. Parasites on the healthy body of the class. Sooner or later the dimmer bulbs would be left behind anyway. It was advisable to confront them with the truth as early as possible, rather than giving them another chance after each failure. With the truth that they simply didn't meet the conditions required to become a fully-fledged member of society. What was the point of being hypocritical? Not everyone could do it. And why should they? There were duds in every year. With some, you could be happy if you managed to instil a few fundamental virtues. Politeness, punctuality, cleanliness. It was a shame they'd stopped giving out citizenship grades. Hard work. Cooperation. Contribution. Proof of the shortcomings of the present educational system.

The later you left getting rid of a failure, the more

dangerous he became. He started harassing his fellows, and making unjustified demands: for decent school-end grades, a positive assessment, possibly even a well-paid job and a happy life. The result of many years of intense support, short-sighted benevolence and reckless generosity. Nobody who gulled the hopeless cases into believing they belonged should be surprised if they eventually came marching into school with pipe bombs and small-calibre firearms to avenge themselves for all the things that had been promised them and repeatedly withheld. And then the candlelit processions.

Lately everyone had started insisting on self-realisation. It was ridiculous. Nothing and no one was fair. Certainly not society. Only nature, perhaps. Not for nothing had the principle of selection made us what we were today: the creature with the most deeply furrowed cerebrum.

But Schwanneke, with her rage for integration, hadn't been able to leave well alone. What could you expect from someone who formed letters out of rows of desks, and semi-circles out of chairs: for a long time a big U, which embraced her desk. Recently it had even been an angular O, so that she was connected with everybody and there was no longer a beginning or an end, just the circular moment, as she once announced in the staffroom. She let the Year Elevens call her by her first name. We're to call her Karola, Inge Lohmark had heard one girl pupil say. Karola! My goodness – they weren't at the hairdresser's!

Inge Lohmark addressed her pupils formally from Year Nine onwards. It was a habit dating back to the days when that was the age when children had officially entered youth. Along with *The Universe, the Earth and Mankind*, and the bunch of socialist carnations. There was no more effective way of reminding them of their own immaturity, and keeping them at arm's length.

The professional relationship didn't involve intimacy or understanding. It was pitiful, if understandable, for pupils to tout for their teachers' favours. Creeping to the powerful. What was unforgivable, though, was the way teachers threw themselves at adolescents. Backsides perched on their desks. Borrowed fashions, borrowed words. Bright scarves around their necks. Dyed blonde strands. Just in order to chum up with the children. Undignified. They relinquished the last scraps of respectability for the brief illusion of fellowship. Leading the way, of course, was Schwanneke with her darlings: cocky little minxes who roped her into breaktime conversations, and broken-voiced youths, for whom she performed the cheapest kind of goggle-eyed, lipsticked sign-stimulus display. Probably hadn't looked in the mirror for ages.

Inge Lohmark had no darlings, and never would. Having crushes was an immature, misguided kind of emotional excitement, a hormonally influenced effusiveness that afflicted adolescents. Having escaped their mothers' apron-strings, but not yet quite a match for the charms of the opposite sex. By way of surrogacy, a helpless member of the same sex or an unattainable adult became the target for half-formed emotions. Blotchy cheeks. Sticky eyes. Inflamed nerves. An embarrassing lapse which, in normal cases, resolved itself once the gonads had attained maturity. But of course: people without professional competence would only be able to offload their educational material by means of sexual signals. Ingratiating trainees. So-called 'favourite teachers'. Schwanneke. The way she defended her commitment to the Year Eight idiots at the teachers' conference. Her brow in wrinkles, shouting into the assembled staff with her red-painted mouth: In the end, we need all our pupils! The icing on the cake would have been if she of all people, childless Schwanneke, who had recently been dumped by her husband, had started saying children are our future. Future indeed. These children here weren't the future. Strictly speaking they were the past: Year Nine was sitting in front of her. They were the last class there would be at Charles Darwin Gymnasium, and would be doing their school-leaving exam in four years. And Inge Lohmark was to act as their head of year. Just Year Nine. They no longer needed the letters they used to have, from A to G. Year by year their numbers were dropping like a unit in wartime. They'd only just managed to scrape a class together. Almost a miracle, given that it was the year with the lowest birth-rate in the region. There hadn't been enough of them for the classes below. Not even when word started going around that this meant the end for Darwin, and the teachers at the three regional schools had got together to make generous recommendations for the senior classes at the Gymnasium. The consequence was that any halfway literate child was elevated to Gymnasium status.

There had always been parents who were convinced that

their child should be at the Gymnasium in spite of all advice to the contrary. But by now there weren't even enough parents in the town.

No, these children really didn't strike her as jewels in evolution's crown. Development was something quite different from growth. This was an impressively shocking demonstration of the fact that qualitative and quantitative change occurred quite independently. Nature wasn't exactly lovely to gaze upon, at this undecided threshold between childhood and adolescence. A developmental phase. Adolescent tetrapods. School an enclosure. Now came the bad time, the airing of the classrooms against the smell of this age group, musk and liberated pheromones, confinement, bodies on their way to their final shape, sweat behind the knees, suety skin, dull eyes, unstoppable, burgeoning growth. It was much easier to teach them things before they were sexually mature. And a real challenge to explain what was going on behind their blank façades: whether they were unreachably far in front, or hobbling along behind because serious refurbishment was currently under way.

They lacked any awareness of their condition, let alone the discipline to overcome it. They stared straight ahead. Apathetic, overtaxed, preoccupied exclusively with themselves. They yielded unresistingly to their own inertia. The power of gravity seemed to act upon them with threefold force. Everything was a massive effort. Every spark of energy at the disposal of these bodies was used up by an excruciating metamorphosis no less extreme than the elaborate transformation of a caterpillar

in the chrysalis. Only in the rarest of cases did a butterfly emerge.

Becoming an adult just required these misshapen transitional forms, on which secondary sexual characteristics flourished like tumours. Here, the laborious process of becoming human was played out before you in slow motion. It wasn't only ontogenesis that recapitulated phylogenesis; puberty did, too. They grew. Day in, day out. In spurts and over the summer, so that you had your work cut out even to recognise them again. Compliant girls turned into hysterical beasts, and eager boys into phlegmatic proles. And then there was the awkward rehearsal of partner selection. No, nature wasn't original. But it was fair. It was a condition like an illness. You just had to wait for it to pass. The bigger and older an animal became, the longer its youth dragged on. A human being required a third of its whole lifetime to reach maturity. On average it was eighteen years before a young human being was able to fend for itself. Wolfgang even had to go on paying for the children from his first marriage until they were twenty-seven.

So there they sat, life's absolute beginners. Sharpening pencils and copying down the pyramid on the board, raising and lowering their heads at five-second intervals. Not yet fully formed, but boldly self-evident with a claim to absoluteness that was both shameless and presumptuous. They were no longer children who always needed to follow, and who disregarded personal space on the most threadbare of pretexts, who extorted physical contact and stared at you brazenly like hooligans on the cross-country bus. They were young adults now, already capable of procreation, but still immature, like prematurely harvested fruit. To them, Inge Lohmark was certainly ageless. It was more likely that she just struck them as old. A state that would never change as far as her pupils were concerned. Everyone young grew older. Old stayed old. She was long past the halfway mark. Luckily. At least that meant she would be spared the indignity of changing noticeably before their eyes. And that knowledge made her powerful. They were still all interchangeable, a swarm in pursuit of the minimum standard. But soon they would become perfidiously autonomous; they would pick up the scent and start finding accomplices. And she herself would start ignoring the lame old nags and secretly back one of the thoroughbreds. Once or twice she had been on the right track. There had been a pilot, a marine biologist. Not a bad haul for a small provincial town.

Right at the front crouched a terrified vicar's child who had grown up with wooden angels, wax stains and recorder lessons. In the back row sat two overdressed little tarts. One was chewing gum, the other was obsessed with her coarse black hair, which she constantly smoothed and examined, strand by strand. Next to her, a tow-headed, primary-school-sized squirt. A tragedy, the way nature was presenting the uneven development of the sexes here. To the right by the big windows, a small primate rocked back and forth, open-mouthed, waiting only to mark his territory with some vulgar comment. It was just short of drumming on its chest. It needed to be kept busy. In front of her was the sheet of paper on which the pupils had written their names, scribbles on the way to a legally valid signature. *Kevin*. Of course. How could it be otherwise.

'Kevin!' Kevin started upright.

'Name a few ecosystems in our region!' The boy in front of him smirked. Wait a second.

'Paul, what sort of tree is that outside?' Paul looked out of the window.

'Erm.' A pathetic throat-clearing. Almost pitiful.

'Thank you.' He was provided for.

'We haven't done that,' Kevin claimed. That nothing better occurred to him. A brain like a hollow organ.

'Oh, really?' Now to the whole class. Frontal attack.

'Think about it again, everybody.'

Silence. At last the ponytail in the front row spoke up, and Inge Lohmark obliged. Of course she knew. There was always a little ponytail pony that hauled the class cart out of the mire. It was for these girls that schoolbooks were written. Greedy for pre-packed knowledge. Mnemonic verses that they wrote down in their books with glitter pens. They could still be intimidated by the teacher's red ink. A stupid instrument of apparently boundless power.

She knew them all. She spotted them immediately. She'd had pupils like this by the cart-load, by the class-load. Year after year. They didn't need to flatter themselves that they were special. There were no surprises. Only the cast changed. Who was playing this time? A glance at the seating plan was enough. Naming was all. Every organism had a first name and a surname: type, species. Order. Class. But for now she just wanted to consider their first names.

Jennifer Dyed blonde hair. Thin lips. Precocious. Selfish from birth. No prospect of improvement. Unscrupulously ample, competition bosom.

Saskia Without make-up possibly even pretty. Regular features, high forehead, plucked eyebrows and moronic expression. Obsessive grooming.

Laura Outgrown, colourless fringe over saggy eyelids. Teary expression. Pimply skin. Lacking in ambition and interest. Unnoticeable as weeds.

Tabea Wolf child in tattered trousers and holey jumpers. Cute face. Feral eyes. Back bent from left-handed writing. Not very promising in other respects either.

Erika The heather plant. Nurtured sadness in sloping posture. Freckles on milky skin. Chewed fingernails. Stringy brown hair. Squint. Firm, slanting gaze. Simultaneously weary and alert.

Ellen Dull, patient beast. Arched brow and rabbit eyes. Face teary from breaktime teasing. Superfluous as a spinster even now. Lifetime victim.

Ferdinand Friendly
but erratic creature. Hollow
eyes. Whorly as an
Abyssinian guinea pig.
Sent to school too young.
Decidedly late-maturing.

Kevin Unclean and boastful.
Uneven fluff on upper lip,
sebaceous complexion. Stupid
but demanding – the worst
possible combination. Only
to be calmed by continuous
feeding. Craves an attachment
figure. Moderately disturbed.
A pain.

Paul Kevin's
bull-necked adversary.
Fast-growing and muscular.
Expressive nature.
Mane-like shock of red hair.
Permanent grin on
bee-stung lips. The classic:
intelligent, but lazy. Hardy
and risk-taking.

Tom Disagreeably
ponderous bodily
presence. Tiny eyes in
obese face. Vacuous expression:
still thoroughly stunned by
nocturnal emission. An olm
would be more attractive. Little
hope that the unfortunate
proportions can be corrected by
further growth.

Annika Brown
ponytail, boring face.
Over-ambitious. Joyless
and industrious as an ant.
Desperately keen
to read out papers. Class
representative from birth.
Wearing.

Jakob Vicar's child. Typical
front-row student.
Narrow-chested. Squint-
eyed in spite of glasses.
Nervous fingers. Hair thick
as mole-fur. Almost
attractively transparent
skin. At least three siblings.
No side.

That was it. As always: no major surprises. Ponytail was already finished. Hands flat on the table. Eyes fixed mesmerised on the board.

Inge Lohmark stepped over to the window. Into the soft morning sun. How good that felt. The trees had already started to change colour. Decomposed chlorophyll made way for bright leaf pigments. Carotinoids and xanthophylls. The long-stemmed leaves of the chestnut, devoured by leafminer moths, were yellow-edged. Strange that the trees worked so hard with leaves from which they would soon be parted anyway. Just like her as a teacher. Same every year. For over thirty years. Always starting over again.

They were too young to value the significance of the knowledge they had acquired together. Gratitude was not to be expected. All that counted here was damage limitation. At best. Pupils were thoughtless creatures. They would all go one day. And she alone would remain behind, hands dry with chalk-dust. In this room, here, between the collection of rolled-up wall charts and the cabinet of visual aids: a skeleton with broken bones, greasy dummy organs with cracks in their plastic skin, and the stuffed badger with burn-holes in its fur, which stared dead-eyed through the panes. Soon they could do that with her. Like that English scholar who wanted to stay connected with his university even after his death. Take part as a mummy at weekly meetings. His last wish was fulfilled. They put clothes on his skeleton. Stuffed it with straw. Embalmed his skull. But something went wrong in the process, so that in the end they put a wax head on his remains. She had seen it when she was in London. Claudia had studied there for a while. Sitting there, in his huge wooden case behind glass. With walking-stick, straw hat and green suede gloves that looked exactly like the pair she had bought in Exquisit in the spring of 1987. For 87 marks. At least Vladimir Ilyich was asleep and could dream of Communism. But those English were still in office. Daily he eyed the students on their way to the auditoria. The display cabinet was his grave. He himself his own memorial. Eternal life. Better than organ donation.

'Old people,' she suddenly began. 'Old people can remember their schooldays even when they've forgotten everything else.' She dreamed repeatedly of her schooldays. Above all her Abitur exam. How she stood there and nothing came to mind. And when she woke up it was always a while before she realised that she had nothing to worry about. She was on the other side, the safe side.

She turned round. Dispirited expressions.

You had to be bloody careful. Before she'd slipped up, they'd discussed all kinds of nonsense in class. Favourite breakfasts. Causes of unemployment. Pet funerals. Suddenly everyone was as bright as a button and the period had flown by. You had to construct hazardous transitions, make your way back hand over hand to the ecosystems where the faces of spirited children immediately drained away again. The weather was the worst. From the weather it was only a cat's leap to personal wellbeing. But they wouldn't find out anything about her. All that helped was to pick up the thread at the very spot where she had lost it. She walked with deliberate slowness back to her desk. Away from the brightly coloured pages. Away from the calamitous weather. Bull by the horns.

'There are cases when patients with Alzheimer's and dementia can't remember the names of their children or their partners, but they can remember their biology teacher's.' Bad experiences sometimes left more of a mark than good ones.

'A birth or a marriage may be an important event, but it does not secure a place in the memory.' The brain, a sieve.

'Never forget: nothing is certain. What's certain is nothing.'

Now she'd even started tapping herself on the head with her forefinger.

The class looked on in dismay.

Back to the book.

'There are about two million species in the world. And if environmental conditions change, they are endangered.'

Total lack of interest.

'Can you think of any species that have died out already?'

A handful of outstretched little arms.

'I mean – apart from the dinosaurs.'

All the hands came down straight away. The nursery disease. They couldn't tell a blackbird from a starling, but they could rattle off the taxonomy of extinct large lizards. Sketch a brachiosaurus out of their heads. Early enthusiasm for the morbid. Soon they'll be playing with thoughts of suicide and haunting cemeteries at night. Flirting with the beyond. More death trend than death drive.

'The aurochs, for example. The Eurasian wild horse,

the Tasmanian tiger, the great auk, the dodo – and Steller's sea cow!'

They had no idea.

'A huge animal that lived in the Bering Sea. A body weighing several tonnes, a small head and vestigial limbs. Its skin was several centimetres thick and felt like the bark of an old oak tree. The sea cow was a quiet animal. It never made a sound. It only sighed briefly when it was wounded. It was tame by nature and liked to come to the shore so that it was easy to stroke. But also to kill.'

'How do you know all that?' Erika, just like that, without putting her hand up.

The question was justified.

'From Georg Steller, a German naturalist. He was one of the last to see them alive.'

Erika nodded seriously. She had understood. What did her parents do? In the past a glance at the class-book would have been enough. Intelligentsia, office workers, manual workers, farmers. Officials to the workers. Pastors to the intelligentsia.

Ellen put her hand up.

'Yes?'

'What did they do with it?' Of course, they'd sniffed out a fellow-sufferer.

'They ate it. It's supposed to have tasted like beef.' A cow is a cow.

But now back to the living.

'And which species are threatened with extinction?'

Five arms went up.

'Apart from panda, koala or whale.'

Again one hand after the other came down. Animal protection for teddy bears. The Bambi effect. Mascots for the cuddly-toy industry. 'A species local to us, for example?'

Total bewilderment.

'There are only about a hundred pairs of lesser spotted eagles in Germany. Some farmers even get money for leaving their fields fallow. Because that way the eagles can pounce more easily on their prey. They live mostly on lizards and songbirds. They lay two eggs, but only one of their young survives.' Correct emphasis. Now they're listening. 'The first chick to hatch kills the next. It pecks away at it for several days. Until the sibling dies and is then devoured by the parents. This is known as innate Cainism.' A glance at the front row. The vicar's son wasn't moving. Had he lost his childhood faith already? More was required for survival than a biblical pair that had once walked on to Noah's Ark. So, once again.

'One sibling kills the other.'

Quiet horror.

'That's not cruel, it's perfectly natural.' Under certain circumstances even killing served to protect the brood.

Now they were alert again. Blood and thunder.

'So why do they even lay two eggs?' Paul. He really seemed to want to know.

'Well, to have one in reserve.' It was quite simple.

'And what about the parents?' Tabea's eyes were wide.

'They watch.'

The signal for break sounded. That was only the start, the first lesson.

Not a bad conclusion. Straight to the point. It didn't ring, it rattled. The bell was still broken. And even before the holidays she'd gone to Kalkowski. Had paid her first visit to his office, which he'd set up in the old boilerman's bunker. The walls, papered with posters of animals. Meticulously tidy desk. And still the smell of coal, even though they'd switched to district heating years ago. She'd asked him to get rid of the piece of cardboard that the Year Thirteens had stuck behind the bell during the last graduation prank. He had leaned back in his worn-out office chair and babbled something about revenge. The revenge of the school-leavers for a wasted year of their lives. He was very serious. He sounded almost like Kattner. All those nature photographs on the wall, and in amongst them the photograph of a bare-bosomed woman. One naked animal amongst many. A janitor was a janitor. But he was right. The new teaching plans, everything changing all the time. Decisions in the regional parliament, the education ministry. Of course it was all to be done over a period of twelve years. Or even ten, if you stripped it down. All that art stuff, for example. But he could still have fixed the bell.

Now they were actually stuffing their books into their bags, with their eyes on the door. But Inge Lohmark went straight into the extension of the period. Important they know what's what. From the very first.

'Please stand up.'

As she said, so it was done. Making the pupils stand up at the beginning and the end of the class was a signal that had been preserved, a reinforcement of the bell. Her teaching method consisted of a series of measures that had formed over the course of her life as a teacher, and become increasingly specialised. Sooner or later experience replaced all knowledge. Only that which was preserved by practice was true.

'On Thursday . . .' she took a deep breath to prolong the moment still further '. . . please work on exercises five and six.'

Artificial pause.

'Now you can go.' It sounded merciful. It was supposed to. They immediately raced outside.

Inge Lohmark opened the window. Fresh air at last. The leaves rustled. Campfire air. Someone somewhere was probably burning leaves already. Deep breath. That felt good. It smelled of autumn.

Whenever you thought things wouldn't change, that everything would just go on like that, the next season came round. The natural course of things. Memories came back of their own accord. What had happened last year? Kattner's resignation. Baffled colleagues. What had they expected? That a big academic family would move out here? They would have had to be Mormons. But that incestuous brood would never have got to a grammar school in the first place. And the year before? The first ostriches. Nine animals, which Wolfgang had put different-coloured suspenders on so that he could tell them apart. Nine ostriches in brightly coloured garter belts, running around the field. That had got people talking. Gawpers turned up every day. Eight hens, one cock. By now there were thirty-two animals. A school class. In the old days anyway.

She locked the classroom.

'A touch higher, please.'

That was all she needed. In the corridor, Frau Schwanneke was standing with two Year Elevens. The two boys were pressing a frame to the wall. By the big glass window Schwanneke stood on tiptoes. She was directing them with flailing arms. A short dress over jeans. Catch me, I'm spring-time.

'Yes, that's lovely.' She spread her fingers in the air.

'Ah, Frau Lohmark!' Schwanneke feigned delight. 'I thought we might brighten up the corridor a bit. And given that we started the school year off with Impressionism . . .'

And indeed, a boggy smear hung there on the wall now, in landscape format.

'So I thought . . . Monet's water lilies go so well with your jellyfish.' She clapped her hands. 'I thought your jellyfish could use some company.'

It was quite unbelievable. That she actually dared to nail her herbaceous aquatic plants up on the wall just a foot away from those magnificent medusas. Bad enough that the art room was on the same floor, and the pupils were for ever daubing the corridor with their inky bilgewater. So far she'd respected the boundaries. Karola Schwanneke's wall was on that side of the toilet, Inge Lohmark's wall on this side of the toilet. This was really going too far. But start a war over a few ugly pictures on the very first day of school? Just stay calm. The clever animal bides its time.

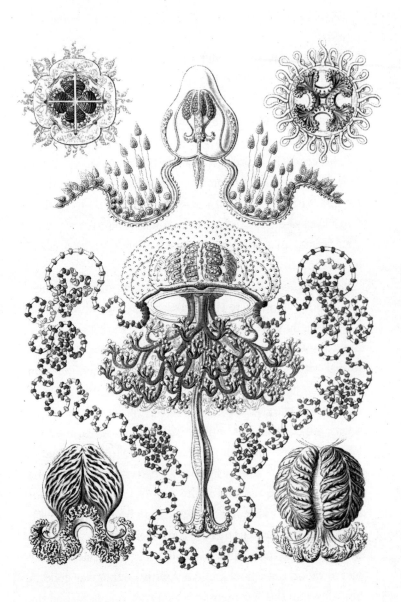

'Haeckel's jellyfish, my dear. They are still Haeckel's jellyfish.'

'The impression is what counts, hence the name. It's about the impression; it has to be really, really immediate.' Schwanneke was really getting into gear now. The two Year Elevens stood there, nodding mutely, not daring to run off for break. All because they were allowed to call her Karola.

The crude horizontal sprawl revealed a hideous shimmer. Spots of mould on musty colours. All rooted in mud, against the background of a pond, a brackish lakelet. Damp, decaying sweetness and a fusty stench. Modern art or not. The beauty of nature didn't need alienation. You could approach it with the utmost precision.

Of what irresistible clarity, what resolute magnificence, on the other hand, were Haeckel's jellyfish; the underview of a helmet jelly, with its curly wreath of lilac rays, its octagonal mouthpipe like a whorly sepal. In the middle, the violet funnel of the discus jelly. Flowing poison hairs spilling from a ruched blue petticoat. Flocking around, its sisters, adorned with crystal stars. And on the right the glazed wonder of the flower jelly, from whose nubby cap two nearly symmetrical tentacles grew. Sweeping garlands, set with red stinging pouches as if with pearls. Framed by two cross-sections. One with the blazing red and white plumage of a Rembrandt tulip, the other as regular as a Caucasian brain.

She had liberated these magnificent pages from the Monograph of the Medusas, a stiff-backed volume that she had found in the school archive. Archive – that was good. A hole down in the basement to which they had banished the tattered wall newspapers, portraits behind glass and thinly framed paintings, canvas prints stretched on plywood. The chubby-cheeked zoo-goer, the young couple on the Baltic beach and the sunflowers bleached by daylight. The walls had suddenly been very bare. Until Kalkowski had put the medusas in silver box frames for her. The sight of them a tonic every day. In the beginning was the jellyfish. Everything else came later. Their perfection remained unattained, no bilaterium could ever be as beautiful. Nothing surpassed radial symmetry.

Enough now.

'Jellyfish live in salt water, water lilies in fresh. Good day to you, Frau Schwanneke.' There was no point arguing with someone who had no sense of true beauty, of genuine greatness.

The little ones had gathered in the playground for morning break. The older teenagers had recently been granted the privilege of staying in their classrooms. Inge Lohmark had been against the idea. After all, fresh air and sunlight were good for the organism at any age. Not least because of the benefits of energy conversion. So only the sixteen-year-olds had gathered around a rubbish bin, below the weathered mosaic showing the crane, the rocket and the short-wave radio receiver. Touching how clumsily they tried to hide their cigarette butts, so much so that she lost the desire to intervene. They even said hello quite nicely. In any case, the supervisor, Frau Bernburg, was a chain-smoker herself, but there was no sign of her anywhere. She'd probably had herself written off sick again as soon as the school year started.

The main building was a two-storey seventies block. Viewed from above, it was the shape of a skewed and withered H, as you could tell from an aerial shot that had been put up recently in the secretary's office. Below it in the picture, the classrooms block as a big I, a displaced vermiform appendix. Two tar-grey letters on a sandy background. Bad subsidence. Concrete erosion flourished behind the guttering. The side towards the ramparts was always damp. A few slab paths led like narrow gangways to the brick-red rectangle of the sports hall. On the wall beside the door to the main building it said in sprayed red letters: Darwin's dying out!

There was nothing now to commemorate Lilo Herrmann. They'd wanted to get everything right back then, and disposed of the old name along with the plywood pictures. Renamed the so-called Extended Secondary School, even before Friendship Between Nations Square and Wilhelm Pieck Street. Lilo Herrmann was long gone now. Another four years and it would all be over, for her too. Inge Lohmark had no illusions about that. Start again somewhere else? Not her. You don't transplant an old tree. And she was a woman, not a tree – and not a man either. Kattner had fathered another child. So they said, anyway. With a former pupil, just after the Abitur exam. All good and legal. Probably nothing in it. Didn't matter anyway. A man in the prime of life. Same age as her. Old bastard. All things being equal she would make it to eighty or ninety. That was even a statistical probability. She was part of the pink bump in the age pyramid in the annual demographic reports, demonstrating the declining birth-rate and the alarming surplus of the elderly: from fir tree to beehive. From beehive to funeral urn. Sprouting and flourishing in peacetime. War dip and pill dip. Let's see your feet. Eighty, ninety years' life expectancy. All the things we expect from life. And in the end so much expectation left over. What was she supposed to do with all that extra time? Sit and wait? She wouldn't get bored. She never got bored. But starting something else all over again? What was it supposed to be? Something new? Okay, then, old tree. Old as a tree. Fifty-five rings, different widths. Early wood and late wood. Changing growth conditions. Wrinkles rather than grain. No year like any other. But they all passed. Moving was never an option. Not with Wolfgang and his ostriches. Not now that they were finally breeding. Better if Claudia came back. Been away long enough, after all, gathering her experiences abroad, twelve years now, half an eternity. She wasn't the youngest any more, either. Could slowly make a start on real life. Build a house, for example. There was still room next to the stables, a decent plot of land with a view of the polder meadows. She would call in on her every day, and then they'd have coffee on the terrace and look down at the meadow. Did Claudia even drink coffee? High time she came back.

In the staffroom, Thiele and Meinhard were hunched over their lunch boxes. Said hello with their mouths full. Still pinned up by the teachers' schedule was speccy Lilo. Brave woman, Communist chemist, martyr for the once-right cause. And a newspaper clipping with the photograph of a stupidly grinning child writing the name of that Italian city on a board. Next to that, the programme of evening classes, cuckoos in the nest: the principles of the foundation of existence, slipper-felting, paper-making, philosophising with pensioners. Occupational therapy for the death-bound.

Kattner came into the room, greeted everyone and studied the schedule. Coloured streamers on a wooden board with hooks. A crazy system, which he took two classes off every week to master.

'So, Inge, what are you going to offer? Maybe biology for domestic purposes?' He swapped a few classes around on the schedule. 'A mushrooming course? Or something to combat garden pests?'

'Hello, Kattner.' Let him make his evening-class jokes. He wouldn't drag her out of her shell as easily as that. Yes, she could stay. The Higher Education college would take over the building. A few courses already lurked in the basement. But not her. Other people could do that. Science wasn't supposed to be a hobby. No one wanted to engage with cell structure or the citric-acid cycle. They preferred to look for a famous ancestor, interpret the stars or learn foreign languages. Slide lectures about the Far East. And then see a bit more of the world. When the world was here: the forest, the field, the river, the moor. It all provided a respectable habitat for toothless species. Including a whole lot placed under the protection of the environment ministry. Even some of which only individual specimens had been found, so rare were they. Every now and again new species appeared, too, uninvited guests, illegal immigrants. The raccoon dog from Siberia. An omnivore. A carrion-eater. Looked like a raccoon, and took over the setts and earths of badgers and foxes. Introduced diseases and drove domestic species out of their ecological niches. Their reproductive success was huge, because both parents looked after the young.

They all cheerfully reproduced. Her own kind didn't, though. Instead they acted as if it was all over in this term, as if the future was going to take place somewhere else, somewhere out there, beyond the Elbe, the border, the continent. They all grasped some scrap of reality that they claimed not to see anywhere around here. As if there were no life in this place. But life was everywhere. Even in stale rainwater.

In the end it was all the fault of the weather. Not least the fact that her daughter stayed over there. The way she'd put it: *Once you've got used to the sun, Central Europe is ruined for you.* Central Europe. The sound of that. The change of location, the change of air, the climate was overrated. But it wasn't as if they were all tubercular, was it?

They all got the hell out. They hadn't grasped a thing. If you wanted to understand the world, you had to start at home. Our home. From Cape Arkona to the Fichtelberg.

There was no skill in clearing off. She had always left that to the others. There had been a short time when she'd toyed with the idea. But that was ages ago. She had stayed. Freedom was overrated. The world had been discovered, most species identified. You could safely stay at home.

'No, old Lohmark will probably go to Yank-Land to be with her daughter. Watch the grandchildren playing from the rocking chair on the porch.' Kattner, still fiddling with the schedule.

Nice try.

At least Meinhard and Thiele made room for her when she joined them. Amazing, though, how quickly Meinhard had settled in. A young man with a mother's body. Maths trainee. Belt a hand's-span too high. A clumsy, sanguine type with red cheeks and bum-fluff on his upper lip, not enough for a moustache. Under his light-coloured shirt, buttoned up to the top, two pointed breasts stood out. A case for the andrology clinic. Something about him was unfinished, and always would be.

Thiele, on the other hand, with his sharp outlines, his narrow, hewn face, a few cracked wrinkles around his mouth. He wore his greying hair combed back, and in spite of his frayed Lenin beard he was neatly turned out. Like many Communists he looked almost aristocratic. Always concerned. But determined to watch the decline of his house with great serenity. He usually withdrew to his cubbyhole, a box-room for map stands and educational materials, which he had commandeered as his office. His Politburo. He smoked imported cigarillos and went on waiting for the global revolution. He was always making noises, his peristalsis rumbled. His gaunt body was an amplifier for the worries that lay in his path.

'It's the plague.' Typical Thiele. Always mumbling something into his philosophical beard.

'What is?' Meinhard didn't understand.

'Today's plague.' Thiele stared at the table top. Poor old thing.

'A hundred men for every seventy women.' He looked up.

'You see? They can choose the best.'

His wife had left him. She had crossed over to the West in the days of the GDR. But now he pretended he was the victim of a demographic shift. One of the thirty men with no woman left over. Condemned to bachelorhood. Mostly food from tins, on the brink of despair. Forced to stuff his dirty laundry in the machine all by himself.

'The rest could turn gay.' Kattner again. He joined them with a broad grin. He looked a bit tired from his holidays. Below his crew-cut a face that still left no impression on her. He started rolling up his sleeves. Strangely brown forearms appeared. Kattner, the whizz kid, the perseverance man, the cold-blooded creature. No one had wanted the job. He had taken pity. And over the years the sociology teacher who had come here to teach them democracy had turned into an alpha beast. The transitional head had become a genial enforcer who kept the show on the road, for as long as the show existed. He had run the school for fifteen years, and he even seemed to enjoy manoeuvring it out of play. He even claimed that this was a stroke of good luck for everybody. For him, perhaps. His adventure playground. Kattner still had something up his sleeve, two plan Bs. A little house, a divorce, two wayward children. Perhaps even three, if there were any truth to the rumours. Uptight, but not a child of woe. Basically it didn't matter who ran the show down. The last one out turned the lights off.

'A third of the population died of the plague, 1565. This is the new plague.' As if that had anything to do with anything. But with Thiele everything was a lesson.

'Thiele, you could really do something on local history.' He shouldn't get so excited. She stroked his blotchy hand. Soft as young leather.

'Thirty per cent. That's easily enough to win you an election.' Meinhard. Probably trying to change the subject.

'Yes, people.' Kattner rubbed his hands. He was in a chatty mood again. You could see that straight away. 'This is a school on the way down. But we're not here to oversee its end, we're making this school sustainable.' Of course: death was also a part of life. 'Dying landscapes aren't all that new or dramatically unique. Schools will close elsewhere too. In the West as well. In the Ruhr. Half of Lower Saxony is empty. It's a universal development. Never heard of rural flight?' So he thought they needed remedial teaching. 'You might even say that the East is still doing well. At least they've put some investment in it. All those new street lights, the motorway . . .'

'But they calculated that the motorway isn't even worth investing in, because there's far too little traffic.' Apparently Meinhard also read the papers.

'Yes, people aren't coming here, they're going away. They should have built a one-way street.' Final destination Vorpommern. An allocated habitat.

'It's insane.' Thiele cleared his throat and stretched. 'Leaving your city used to be a punishment. Being banished was the worst thing that could happen to you.' He looked up. 'Now it means you're one of the winners.'

Kattner bit into a carrot and leaned back. 'The Martenses just needed to try a bit harder, and then we'd have been sitting pretty.'

'The Martenses?' Meinhard could look really stupid sometimes.

'Like rabbits . . .' Kattner stuck the carrot into his fist. 'But no matter. Three families like that and we'd have been saved. We'd have had classes right through to retirement. But no! Anyone who passes their exams is frigid.'

'You mean infertile.' Meinhard suffered from teacheritis too. The urge to correct.

'Oh, it boils down to the same thing.'

'Well, you've taken a lot of trouble to make sure it's enough. But you should have started a bit earlier.'

That hit home. Kattner leaned forward again. Ready to pounce.

'Listen, Frau Lohmark. We had to re-evaluate everything. We all had internships. Not just you.'

Oh, that old thing again. The age of the interloper was over once and for all, the age of the know-all who put a chair in the corner and wanted only to be a fly on the wall, as the last intern, that goateed dolt from the education office, had put it with a jovial smile. But that fly had been a wasp which had dared to criticise their lessons. *Frau Lohmark teaches frontally* it said in the report. And what do you suggest, Clever-Clogs? In circles, like Schwanneke? Working in groups, perhaps? The children messed about like idiots. Looked at their bogeys through the microscope, rather than onion skins. And mourned the paramecia in the hay infusion when they finally tipped the stinking broth down the bog. And anyway they copied their results from whoever the current ponytail happened to be.

Their lessons needed to be more realistic, she was told after that. What nonsense! Biology was realistic anyway. The theory of life, its laws and phenomena, its proliferation in time and space. A science of observation that addressed all the senses. But that was typical again. First they scrap the killing of animals for dissection classes, then they demand more realism!

All the things that were forbidden these days. Animal experiments, my eye. What was cruel about those! The animals were dead! Objects of study. Purposes of research. Experiments. Having a fertilised egg incubated by infrared light. Opening it to see the heartbeat. Lamp off. Proof delivered. The African clawed frog that recognises pregnancy. Spawning females injected with women's urine. Plaque in the Petri dish. The twitching of the amputated frog's leg. Still wet. The muscles they touched with silver and iron. Two metals, noble and base, from the far-away galvanic series. Proof produced. The neural pathway a conduction of stimuli. An electrical circuit. Chemical energy could be

turned into electrical energy. Nature spoke through the experiment. But no: now you were only allowed to open up the bellies of dead fish. But herring went off quickly. And trout were expensive. At least cows' eyes were still allowed, but because of mad cow disease pigs' eyes were preferable. She loved that moment, when the lens fell on the spread-out newspaper and enlarged a word in the article. Then everything fell silent at last. The children forgot their revulsion and raptly admired the iridescence of the retina. Of course it was all about vividness. But it wasn't every day that they came across the grasping reflex, earthworms hell-bent on regeneration, or Pavlov's drooling dogs. There were dioramas in the natural history museum. Formalin preparations, fluorescent bones and flashing buttons. You couldn't beat teaching from the front. Her lessons were good. Her pupils were good. Certainly: some of them were afraid of her. Her assessments always came out of the blue, but word got out, so they were usually prepared. She was almost always the one who determined what she taught. And the teaching plan: the spiral curriculum. From the simple to the complex. Themes recurring in ever more complicated form. Like a slowly tightening vice. What mattered was the result. And her results were good. Her grade overview was above the regional average. Still. Of course she'd been lucky. Biology and sport. The pursuit of life. The sciences didn't need to be rewritten. They weren't about thought and opinions. They were about observation and investigation, definition and explanation! Hypothesis, induction, deduction. Natural laws were international. Thiele and Bernburg had had plenty to chew on with the new facts and data. A few boundaries fewer, still. But biology. That was a fact. And biology lessons were a documentary report. It communicated no knowledge that was then rendered invalid by being shifted to a different political system. The world could only be described and explained on the basis of itself. And the laws to which it was subject had unrestricted validity. Nothing needed to be voted on. It was a true dictatorship!

'Meinhard, you know how you can tell the Martens children?' Kattner leaned forward. 'By their gnawed faces.' The glee with which he stroked his cheek.

'Oh, enough of the horror stories.' He just couldn't let it be. And it had been long before his time anyway. Such a freeloader with other people's stories.

'They wanted a shithouse. At their farm. They just stuck a pipe in the cellar. And that was their little bower. Their shithouse bower. Until the rats came. First into the cellar, then up the stairs, into the children's room. And there were enough children there . . .'

There were various reproductive strategies. K-strategists invested a lot of time and effort in a few descendants, r-strategists little in many. Simple calculation: quality versus quantity. The goal was the increase in their likelihood of survival. It was like betting: either you staked everything on a single card. Or you spread your wager. And even if two of the Martens progeny had been left with truly ugly scars that looked like birthmarks, they were still alive. 'At least our colleagues at the special school still have a few years' work to be going on with.'

Kattner sighed. His way of winning their confidence. Warning and concealment.

'Ah, do you remember? When allied subjects still sat at a single table . . .' Now it was the turn of the fraternisation tactic. Communal showering. 'Every man for himself. At the window, the cackling art and German teachers, then the sad geographers and historians, the sinking sports teachers, the elegant maths and physics faction over here by the case with the cups in it.' He pointed to the trophies, paused. What a display. 'We could usefully give those a clean, Lohmark.'

'Yes, we could.' As if she hadn't said exactly that before the holidays.

'All right then. And now, look around you! All gone. Just two tables left. Science here, humanities over there. Here the facts, there the fiction. Here the reality, there the interpretation.' Drum roll, fanfare. 'The school isn't dying, it's concentrating on the essential!' He struck the table and frowned. Hats off. Maybe he even believed what he was saying. 'But we just don't talk enough.' They were in a school, after all, not at the Party convention. 'This is a unique chance.' He hadn't even nearly finished. As at the weekly meetings, when he liked to pick a fight and pass it off as democratic further training. Someone was always allowed to say anything. And they were all right. Peace, joy, and universal bladderhood. Everything could be contradictory. And nothing meant anything at all.

No one was up to the truth: the existence of a single, verifiable, provable reality. Certainly not these men, who had stayed on at school out of fear of real life, and who puffed themselves up in front of adolescents behind closed doors. The strutting of those eternally held back another year. You had to take the world as it was. Not the way you wanted it to be.

'I promise you: we will be competitive. We will make this school sustainable. Together. With the pupils. We need more commitment. Outside of lessons, too. That's why I've decided to deliver an address every week. Motivational training. To reinforce our cohesion. A speech about the future. What do you think of that? A kind of bugle call. You're familiar with that.'

He was going completely round the bend now. There was probably move to come, too. Next would come slogans and class goals. The stagehand wanted to preach. Read the requiem. The whole programme.

'Lohmark, you're right. Once a month. Monday. No! Mid-week's better. On Wednesday! During morning break. On the first Wednesday of every month. That's how we'll do it.'

'Who is Lilo Herrmann again?' Pointedly cheerful.

'A German labour fascist.' Thiele's answer, very dry, not looking up. A pupil was supposed to have given that answer in an exam, more than twenty years ago. Not as a provocation, out of pure stupidity. It was Thiele's best joke. Kattner liked to share it. His weakness for local anecdotes, which he would have been wiser to avoid. But he secretly regretted not having been there. Was proud when people thought he was from around here.

Kattner tapped Thiele's sleeve.

'Comrade, we'll have to have a chat about your Politburo. It can't go on like this.'

Thiele said nothing. Kattner let him go. At the door he turned again.

'So: have a good game! And long live fresh air!' He waved and disappeared. The school really was a sinking ship. There wasn't even any point rowing any more. They were all just defending their own careers. And what else were they left with, but to assign some sort of meaning to the random, inevitable sequence of events? Marriage, the inevitable birth of the first child, and almost inevitably of the second. Thiele, a doughty injun, had even squeezed a third out of his wife. Communists had three, vicars four or five and anti-social types six and counting. How many children the Martenses had by now no one knew exactly. She had once asked one of the Martens children, when the backward pupils still took the same bus to town as everyone else. He promised to ask when he got home. Then, the next time, the child counted its siblings off on its fingers. He needed the fingers of three hands. There were thirteen of them, at the time at least. With the babies of the two oldest sisters, fifteen, even. Like organ-pipes. Thirteen. That was more than she had in her class now.

She had just one child, an only. And that child was so far away that it didn't really count. She was probably a C-strategist. The danger of extinction was great when the birth-rate was so low. What was the point of a child on the other side of the world? When the time difference meant the child was so far away, nine whole hours, more than half a day? One of them was always ahead of the other. You could never tell who of whom. It was impossible to share so much as a moment. The Martenses had enough in reserve if one of them fell under a bus. But one child. It was all or nothing.

In her room in the sports hall everything was exactly as she had left it before the holidays. On the table lay her whistle and stopwatch. The curtains were closed. Pleasant gloom.

How tired she was all of a sudden. Sit down. Just for a minute. Rest her head against the wall. In the mirror above the washbasin part of her head. Her forehead. Her wrinkles. Her hairline, the hair grey, for over twenty years. Deep breaths for a few minutes. The blue-green tracksuit in her lap. Legs bare, cheesy pale, as if there hadn't been a summer. Her palms felt cool on her thighs. The warmth surged up in waves. To her head. Over her eyes a flicker and suddenly sweat. A textbook hot flush. But it wasn't in a textbook. They didn't actually learn about that. No one told them about the body's second transformation. Creeping renaturation. Atrophy of the uterus. Discontinuance of the period. Dry vagina. Faded flesh. It was only ever about blossoming. Autumn. My goodness. Yes, it was autumn. Rustling leaves. Where would a second spring come from now? The idea was ridiculous. Bringing in the harvest. Fetching in the fishing-nets. Thanksgiving mood. Anticipation of the pension. Evening of life. Mists and mellow fruitfulness. But

where did that weariness come from? The weather, or the
first day of school?

She had woken up last night. It couldn't have been four
in the morning. It was still pitch dark. A draught brushing
her cheek. Once. Again. Her pulse straight to one hundred
and eighty. A flutter. A big moth? A privet hawk moth, but
it was actually too late for them. She had had to feel around
for the switch of her bedside lamp. When the light came on
at last, the creature flew frantically around the room. Flew
big loops. Imaginary figures of eight, a foot below the ceiling. Ghost-train fluttering. A bat! A lost young pipistrelle.
Its radar system had failed, its infallible sense of orienta-
tion had abandoned it. Its mouth was open, it was
screaming. But its screams were inaudible.

Its intelligence might be enough to tell it to fly through
angled windows and tell that this wasn't a crack in a barn
wall, not a hollow in a tree, not a hole in the masonry of a
power station, but not to find its way back out through the
chink of a window. It must have come from one of the day
roosts that were now disbanding at summer's end. Every
animal was on its own. In search of a new home.

She had turned out the light, and gone quietly down to
the cellar. For safety's sake she had pulled the blanket over
her head. A good thing Wolfgang slept so soundly. He
would have been startled by the sight of her. A ghost on its
nocturnal rounds. She could still hear his snoring as she
stood by the shelf with the Kilner jars.

Then everything went very quickly. The creature probably sensed that there was no way out. A few times it tried

to bolt, but when she tried to tip the jar over its little body, it surrendered out of sheer terror. It looked as if it was dead. Stuffed. Very fragile: thick, brown mouse-fur. Small, crooked claws. Leathery wing-tips. The fine flying membrane. Protruding red limbs. The black barbed hook of its outstretched thumb. The flat head. A wet, gleaming snout. Tiny vampire teeth. The horrified mouth of a newborn. Hard, anxious eyes. So much anxiety. They were closer to humans than they were to mice. The same set of bones: humerus, radius, ulna and carpus. In the funnel-shaped ears, the same cartilage. And identical sex organs. A pair of nipples at breast height. Free-hanging penis. One or two young per year. And at birth they were almost completely naked.

She had wondered briefly whether she could use the bat in her lesson. Present it to the new class as a typical synanthropic species. The smallest of all mammals. But then she wanted to get rid of the creature as quickly as possible. She opened the window. And then the jar. The animal crawled out very slowly, fell a short distance at first, then caught itself, spread its wings and vanished into the darkness, somewhere in the direction of the garage. She quickly closed the window and went back to bed. It was light by the time she fell asleep.

The girls were cackling in the corridor. Time to get going. She straightened herself, got dressed and went outside to muster them all.

'Stand still!'

The line was uneven.

'Chests out, bottoms in!'

Two girls had to swap places before the disintegrating line was correct again and then they were standing neatly, in order of height. It was important to keep track of things.

'Ready to play! Three rounds to warm up, no shortcuts! You know I have eyes everywhere.'

It was good to be outside.

'Come on! Off you go!'

The girls started running, impelling their young but already sluggish bodies across the playground, and disappeared behind the main building towards the city ramparts.

Hard to believe that these were the ones who were supposed to have established themselves in the evolutionary competition. Selection really was blind. She was more than three times as old as these bed-wetters, but she was in far better shape. She would have won by miles against them. They lacked any kind of basic tension. Awkward motor actions. Wobbly padding. You wouldn't get anywhere with this lot. But then these days you didn't get squads of girls turning up to take one of the horses out of Lohmark's stable. It had been different once. The roll of honour still hung by the entrance to the sports hall. She had insisted on that. So that they could all see what records were: yellowing numbers. Sports day in those days: spikes under running shoes smuggled over the border. Freshly whitewashed lines on the red cinder track. Voices from loudspeakers. To your places. On your marks. Get set. Muscles tensed. Bang. The start was everything. Gold, silver, bronze. Shiny cardboard on red gift-wrap ribbons. How many of those she had at home. A whole drawerful. Sinewy children's bodies, stretching towards the finishing line and then dipping forwards across it, as they'd seen on television. Back then she had produced a whole series of winners in the local Spartakiad, and even one winner in the regional Spartakiad. Always an eye for who was fit, aside from the accepted athletic wisdom. Pole vaulters and gymnasts have to be small, basketball players, on the other hand, have to be huge, and you could only be a decent swimmer if you had big arms and extra-large feet. That was one thing. But she immediately saw who was willing to submit all her interests to a strict training regime. Anyone humble and disciplined enough to win in the competition at some point. Years could pass before that happened. It was a matter of guiding different propensities on to purposeful tracks. Turning potential talents into winners. Today you could consider yourself lucky if you persuaded the girls not to call in sick when they had their periods. The idea that they dared to hold world championships when so many talents remained unrecognised. But what counted was the result, not the potential.

The first of them came trickling back, red-faced, into the playground.

It started to rain, hesitantly and silently. They immediately put on their protesting faces. No discussion. Brief reminder of the beneficial effects of toughening up. Run-up, then landing in the damp sand. Some of the Graces complained about a few leaves on the short track. As if they were on their way to an Olympic Gold. And then, once the track had been cleared, trotting listlessly off without the slightest sign of effort. They let themselves slump into the sand like wet sacks. So that was the future. No sign of fitness fanaticism. These were the mothers of future generations. Theoretically, at least. Just because they still had everything ahead of them, they could let themselves go like this.

Another eight weeks until the autumn break. She turned the key in the ignition several times. The car emitted nothing but a hoarse rattle. She got out and opened the boot, but there was nothing obviously wrong. Wolfgang said she needed a new car anyway. She didn't. It must have been the battery. That had happened a few times before. And on the first day of school. Fine. On the bus, then. She left the car where it was and walked to the bus stop. Three columns of numbers on the timetable. Midday. Afternoon. Evening. The number one. The four and the six. After that, nothing. There was still time until the one o'clock bus set off.

She took the beaten path across the weedy patch of lawn behind the sports hall up to the embankment, and walked a little way under the chestnut trees, along the broken rampart. The weathered bricks gleamed damply, and on the wet ground the leaves, fat with rain, pointed pinnate fingers into the air. In the puddles the spiny fruit lay burst. Evaporation and precipitation. The natural cycle. Water on its way to the sea.

It wasn't easy to tell which of the city houses on the Ring were still inhabited. All with a view of the green countryside, of the ramparts. And of the moat, a nameless, stinking watercourse. Gaps in the row of houses. Smeary nineteenth-century buildings next to half-plastered façades. Windows boarded shut with plywood. The impression of a demolished house in a firewall. The walls covered with slogans: Wealth for all. Fuck off *Wessis*.

Only the gate from the brick gothic past defied decay. And it had survived the Thirty Years' War. But this wasn't a war. This was capitulation. A woman came towards her along the high road. Older than her. Spherical belly. Waxy face. Her cigarette-yellow hair knotted in a bun. Under her arm a big square envelope full of X-rays. She was one of those people who only change their underwear because they're afraid they might end up in hospital. An accident. You never knew. At her age. She gave her a penetrating, almost challenging look. Just don't respond. Blank face. Lesser spotted eagle-eye. And if they were both the last people in the world, Frau Lohmark wouldn't say hello. What did she care about someone else's misery? Let the old woman look elsewhere if she craved human contact.

In the market in front of the town hall there were, as usual, a few all-day drinkers. Plainly they still had to drink away what remained of their reason. One of them was standing on the little patch of lawn, pissing against a shrub. The old children's trick: if I can't see them, they can't see me. His field of vision shrank to the range of his stream of urine. The free-hanging penis, priority of primates. Impressive, the concentratedly casual way in which the business was done. Shamelessly obvious. Free as an animal. A bigger sexual organ as compensation for the missing tail. Certainly men were sad that they couldn't lick their own organs the way dogs do. But at least they could hold on to them with both hands. Just the two of them, a whole life long. The inequality of the sexes. The absence of the second X chromosome. There could be no compensation for that. With unembarrassed awkwardness he buttoned up his trousers and tottered back to his bottle. Not a delta alcoholic. More of a binge drinker. Hope dies last of all.

Besides, the city, or what was left of it, was slipping into its midday sleep, quiet and unreal, like everything abandoned by human beings. People used to warn of the danger of overpopulation. Since then there must have been a few billion more on the planet. No sign of that here, though.

Like that ghost town that they'd been to see in the Mojave desert. In the scorching midday sun of a particularly hot California summer day. They'd even paid to get in. The only time she and Wolfgang had been over there to visit Claudia. Must have been ten years ago. She'd said at the time that she'd be coming back soon, that she just wanted to finish this one course and show her parents where she'd been living for the last year. They'd really believed it. All of them.

By the gate into the city, a board with population figures. From the city's foundation to its end. From a few hundred to nil. An enamelled washbasin in the tiny museum, laid out as if it were a find from the Messel Pit. A brochure with the CVs of the former inhabitants, written in peculiar German. Barely comprehensible scraps of sentences. Europeans who had come here in trekking parties. Or alone. They'd left their homes for the view of a few lumps of precious metal. Hard labour in the clods where others had already found gold, silver, copper or borax. Nothing was as dangerous as leaving your natural habitat. The idea that man didn't even stop at the desert! His tolerance curve was really quite considerable. He could survive almost anywhere. And constantly had to prove as much, as if obeying some sort of compulsion. Flaunting his ecological potency. Ants needed thousands of species to colonise the whole world, while humanity managed it with only a handful of varieties.

The schoolhouse stood a little way apart. A little half-timbered building that had been rebuilt half-life-sized, for some unfathomable reason. The inside like an enlarged doll's house. A map of the world above the board. In the middle America, Eurasia separated off and forced to the edges. One part on the left, one on the right. Greenland was enormous. A whole country the size of Africa. On the walls, signs with the many regulations for the teachers: No smoking. No ice-cream. Wear at least two petticoats. When she came back out into the light, she saw all the emergency generators that provided the desert backdrop with electricity, souvenir stalls and gemstone shops everywhere. Even though the wooden posts to which horses had once been tied still stood, even though behind the ghost town the entrances to the old silver mine ate like mouse-holes into the stony desert, with the best will in the world she couldn't imagine real people ever living here, people whose remains now lay beneath the pile of gravel that was the graveyard. It could only be a mock-up, a mock-up village in the middle of a dusty, stony desert framed by the mountain panorama. And to think she'd paid money to see it. No, history really wasn't her subject. And natural history didn't seem to come into it very much here. The desert might have been geologically interesting and an important habitat for a handful of animals and plants. But the complete absence of chlorophyll was profoundly disturbing.

This town here would never recover from its population dip. And no one would later pay money to come and see it. A city in the back end of Pomerania, with nothing left to offer but the seat of the district administration. On the narrow river a harbour for scrap and bulk materials, a sugar refinery and a museum. The market a car park. One or two rows of historic buildings. The unsteepled church a huge rudiment of brick gothic. The centre itself full of new constructions, Residential Building Plan number 70, plainest execution, no clinker or gravel in the exposed aggregate concrete. First they had been renovated. Now most of them were empty. The new motorway on their doorstep, just half an hour away. Twenty miles away it turned off sharply to the west. But at least something grew here: a battalion of pansies outside the shopping arcade. A regiment of violets, the latest prettification measure by the occupational therapy patients. Common ivy, caught up in the balconies of the tarted-up façades of the new buildings. And there were huge amounts of plants that had made their way into this estate with no human assistance. They flourished gloriously and almost unnoticed: the goose-grass that occupied every square inch of undeveloped ground. The old agrimony that had worked its way here from the edge of the fields, to the marketplace, the centre of the town. Lowly knotweed spilled from the cracks in the cobblestones. Not to mention the common dandelion, the universal flower that marked every street corner with bristling potency. The wild vegetation was everywhere. The felty white leaves of the common wormwood. The leafy carpet of the chickweed. Ineradicable goosefoot. An astonishing wealth of species. Above all on Steinstrasse, where ruins alternated with empty old buildings. Houses in very different stages of decay. Stop. Hadn't Frau Bernburg once lived here? The bell had been pulled out, the signs were illegible. The door was open. Cool air came up from the cellar. An immortelle even blossomed in the courtyard. Leggy yarrow on a heap of rubble. The false ears of wall barley with their long beards. Weeds didn't wither.

Here, only things that flourished survived. Far from the carefully tended decorative beds, cosseted allotments and other meticulously cared-for secondary biotopes. Disc mayweed, hardwearing pearlwort, sly wildrye, stubborn vegetation. It was propagation that secured existence. Complex pollination operations were successful here. It had to happen quickly. Before pesticides could touch them, the weeds had already multiplied. The sticky seeds of the tough-leaved lamb's foot stuck to the sole of everyone's shoes. Sweet brake tossed out its tiny spores. The dandelion let its parachutes sail. Seeds carried on the wind. Shepherd's purse could pollinate itself if need be. The plants themselves, however, had no plans to move. They had no choice but to stay where they were. And they made the best of it. They infiltrated any free areas, occupied unused interstices, germinated in pavement cracks, in masonry fissures, rooted in the dirty earth of the piles of

rubble, dug into the spilled remains of earlier constructions. Lime, cement, mortar. They didn't care. On the contrary. Even the driest, most calcareous soil was fertile enough for the hard-nosed representatives of the green front.

Sprouting plants were underestimated. Even as a student she hadn't been able to warm to greenery. Servile toilers in the photosynthesis factory. To be defined in countless scientific exercises. It was always a matter of counting. How many leaves they had, how many stamens. Horsetails, ferns and pinewood bracken, gymnosperms, dicotyledons, monocotyledons, legumes and brassicas, mints and asters. Alternate, basal and decussate. Fruit. Food, medicine, ornament. The individual organs of photosynthesis. Feeding the circulation, the motor of the metabolism. Plants turned energy-poor materials into energy-rich. Animals did the reverse. We just weren't autotrophic. Day after day, in every little leaf, in every tiny chloroplast, the miracle that kept us all alive occurred. Epidermis, cuticle, spongy mesophyll. If you were green you wouldn't have to eat anything, you wouldn't have to go shopping, you wouldn't have to work. You wouldn't have to do anything at all. You would just have to lie in the sun for a bit, drink some water, absorb carbon dioxide, and everything, really everything, would be fine. Chloroplasts beneath the skin. It would be wonderful!

Mute, patient vegetation. Hats off to it. Plants could communicate without language, and were sensitive to pain even without a nerve system. Supposedly they even had feelings. Perhaps that was why they were superior to us, because they got by without feelings. Some plants had more genes than human beings did. The most promising strategy for the seizure of power lay in being underestimated. Before striking at the right moment. You couldn't ignore the fact that flora lay in wait. In ditches, gardens and greenhouse barracks they waited for their deployment. Soon they would take everything back. With their oxygen-producing tentacles they would take control of the abused territories, defy the weather, burst tarmac and concrete with their roots. Bury the remains of the past civilisation under a solid covering of leaves. It was only a matter of time before everything was returned to its original owners.

Nitrogen-hungry stinging nettles feasting on the stony rubble, where soon the woody stalks of the clematis would form an impenetrable thicket. The ground covered with bracken. With splayed leaves. Half fresh, half rotten. Mushrooms, lichen and mosses that flourished even on tarmac. Spurred on for all eternity. A cloak of silence. Everything already bore within it the seed of future nature, future landscape, future forest. Well-tended parks? Troublesome forestry? A greater power was at work here! No one could stop it. Eventually, in just a few centuries, stately mixed woodland would stand here. And of all the buildings, the church at most would remain, hollowed out, a brick skeleton, a ruin in the forest, like in a painting. Wonderful. You had to think bigger, further, beyond the puny human scale. What was time? The Plague, the Thirty Years' War, becoming human, the first fire in the caves of the hominids? It was all just a blink ago. Man was a fleeting protein-based phenomenon. An amazing animal, to be fair, that had afflicted the planet for a short time, and would eventually disappear again. To be replaced by worms, mushrooms and microbes. Or buried under a thick layer of sediment. A funny fossil. Never to be excavated. The plants remained, though. They were there before we were, and they would live on after us. This place was still just a shrinking city, production had been turned off long ago, but the true producers were already at work. This place would not decay, instead it would be overgrown. A proliferating amalgamation, a peaceful revolution. Blossoming landscapes.

The bus was bound to come soon. The pupils had already ganged together at the bus stop. They included a few from her class: Kevin, Paul, Fatty and the two Graces from the dunces' desk. They had their sights on Ellen, the sacrificial victim. Brute force applied. If she went around looking so despondent, she could hardly be surprised. It always took two. She could already hear the wails: Frau Lohmark! Frau Lohmark! Barking up the wrong tree there. If you were a victim, you had only yourself to blame. Pity took six minutes, and Frau Lohmark didn't want to wait that long. And in any case she made it a principle not to talk to pupils outside of lessons. They parted company at midday. This was no longer her territory.

Erika stood a little apart, her rucksack between her feet, her right leg bent, one shoulder higher than the other, her face as asymmetrical as an elm-leaf. From the side, you might almost have thought she was a boy. She was wearing a thin, crumpled raincoat, navy blue. Delicate wrists peeped from white blouse cuffs. Her left hand a half-open fist. Circling chestnuts. She was looking very calmly at something on the other side of the road. But she couldn't possibly read the roll of honour above the entrance from here. And it didn't matter anyway. Her chin seemed to jut. A white patch on her cheek. A stork bite. Where did that come from? A slip of the forceps. A badly healed scar. What did she care? The girl could be her daughter. Nonsense. Her granddaughter. Where did that idiotic thought come from? How had Kattner organised that one? Flattery. How had he won the girl round? She really could be her grand-daughter.

And of course she had a daughter. Sometimes she forgot that she had a child at all. What in heaven's name was Claudia doing over there? It was completely incomprehensible. First of all it had just been about a degree, then a trip, finally about a man and then about a job. First the man disappeared, then the job and over the years all the other reasons as well. Claudia had stopped reacting ages ago when Inge Lohmark asked. And eventually she had stopped asking, to keep the rare telephone conversations from getting even rarer. Every now and then an email arrived. Brief signs of life. Warmest regards. No news. Certainly no answers. The prospect of grandchildren wasn't looking good. Claudia was already thirty-five. Ovulation was no longer as regular as before.

By now they had encircled Ellen. Kevin as ringleader. Fatty grinned broadly and was glad to be allowed to join in. They were shoving her back and forth a bit, and taking her hairband. They were actually too old for that sort of childish behaviour. Pure boredom. She was stupid enough to play along, and ran after them. Hairband in the dirt. Ellen bending down. Kevin shoving her. Couldn't the bus come at long last? If they went on like that she would be forced to step in. Ellen whimpered, closed her eyes and threw her head back. The defence position. But humans lack the bite inhibition.

What curious ears Erika had. Angular concavities. Pronounced cartilage. Odd structure. White fluff on the large lobes.

Erika turned her head and looked at her. Almost outraged. What was up with her? What did she want? That piercing gaze. That superior expression. Why was she staring for such an incredibly long time?

The bus came at last. Everyone jostled forward. Erika dropped her chestnuts and stepped calmly aboard. How conceited she was. Inge Lohmark was careful to be the last one on.

After a few minutes they had left the town centre and were driving through the suburbs. Past abandoned industrial units, garage buildings under flat roofs, the allotment colony and the big supermarket car parks. Soon they were on the thoroughfare into the hinterland. A big sign by the edge of the road: NOT A PLACE TO DIE. Wooden crosses and dirty soft toys in the ditch told a different story.

On the right, the failed attempt to convert an old railway carriage into an American diner. On the left the old farm, now run by a few incomers. The city-dwellers couldn't help themselves. They couldn't see that they were merely keeping the area alive artificially, with their imported enthusiasm for the recalcitrant heathland and the bare-brick houses, even for the taciturnity of the natives. They tried it for a few years, complained that they didn't belong there, until it slowly dawned on them that they would never belong there, because things like belonging and community had long since ceased to exist. They wouldn't be bought with organic milk and arts centres. This wasn't a place to die. But neither was it a place to live. Everyone did his own thing. Time to turn off the breathing apparatus. Medical progress. Would they want to be kept artificially alive? As with her mother, after they'd taken out her uterus and her ovaries. As a precautionary measure. But precautionary measures no longer came into it. Noises like an indoor fountain. Gurgling machines. Beeping monitors. Every quarter of an hour her pulse was taken. The shit ran straight into the bag. That was practical enough. Stroking her hand like they do on television. You had to do something. Perhaps she should have signed one of those scraps of paper, a declaration of intent. What were they called again? The bus turned off the main road and looped back to the three villages. Pearls lined up along a paved path. Anything but ornaments. Cars coming in the opposite direction were forced into passing spaces. That was it: a living will. She would do something like that. Should have done a long time ago. You could never know. At her age. Nothing was certain. That was for sure.

Strange, that little dip in the back of Erika's neck between her sloping shoulders. Her unruly hair. Vertebral bumps above her hanging hood. Bones under pale skin. On it the delicate web of the shadows of the leaves: fine welts alternated with rippling clouds. Now she got to her feet. Why was she getting up? Right, the bus was stopping. It was the last of the big farms, a few houses on the edge of the forest. All inhabited. Or at least that was how it looked. Chickens behind a wooden fence. Beware of the dog. Which one did she live in? Did she have brothers and sisters? Was this where she came from? She was the only one who got out. She walked down the road very slowly. Her rucksack dangled from one shoulder. Bad posture programmed in. And already the bus was driving on. Around the bend. No longer to be seen.

A young grasshopper was crawling along the window-pane, spreading its bright green wings. Back and forth, looking for a way out.

She hadn't been on the school bus for years. Everything looked different from up here, almost beautiful: the lime trees along the avenue, leaning from the frayed edges of the tarmac towards the middle of the road. Uncultivated land with mole hills. Channelled ditches, treetops full of mistletoe. On the damp meadows grey birch trees that hadn't survived the last flood. Gappy chicken-wire over collapsing and corrugated-iron sheds. An endless railway crossing, fresh bedding for old tracks. In a field, Holstein cattle stood in churned black soil. Silos gleamed in the distance. A few seagulls mistook the field for the sea. Here and there a tarred path led to a remote farmhouse across crop-rotating fields. Puddles in rubbery tractor trails, mountains of car tyres, old septic tanks, squalid waste dumps. An untidy landscape, mechanically worked, a mosaic of monocultures. Soil scarification. Fertilisation. Edible plants and livestock. Animal breeding and arable farming. The regulated socialisation of organisms to increase yield value. The landscape had been cultivated long ago. The lanky poplars in the village sports ground. The pond with its boxwood trees. Cobblestones. Welcome home. The bus stopped.

By the bus shelter, a few teenagers as usual, killing time. Swearing, smoking, drinking. No wonder none of them had got the hang of Darwin. Or made it into her class. Tarmac covered with little puddles of spit. Boys that age plainly had a special relationship with their spit. The main thing was bodily fluid.

There was a new removal firm in the shopping centre. *Germany wide!* The words were up in sticky letters on the shop window. With an exclamation mark. In the car park, the bright red vans, each one so big that a whole household could fit inside. A life in a lorry. Today you could easily take everything with you. But where to? She would be staying here.

Behind wire mesh, the plot where the big farm had once stood, and the barn that burned down exactly a year after a dermatologist from the Sauerland had done it up at great expense. In the sports ground the little stage for festivities and victory celebrations. Red flags. The smell of lilac, sausages and beer. The mayoress delivering a speech. Her enormous bosom behind the certificate. Firm handshake. With that bust a hug was impossible anyway. Big rising generation. Children all over the place, football matches and the works do. Medals for the grown-ups, badges for the children. Meritorious labour activists. The golden house number for a freshly whitewashed façade. All out for the First of May! For a whole winter Claudia had played with the mayoress's daughter, a pale, quiet girl. Until Claudia had broken a metacarpal with a shard of ice while building an igloo. In the bedroom there were loads of pictures of bosomy women, Claudia had told her. Amazing that she'd told her such a thing! The mayoress's husband was a driver for a drying plant, a great wardrobe of a man. So it was the mayoress who brought her the X-ray. It was just a fracture. Things like that happened when children were playing. They were still living in the new buildings at the time. Two and a half oven-heated rooms. And yes, there, beside the little stage, that was where the siren had been. It went off once a week, just after the post-lunch nap. Even when you were used to it, it was always a shock. That long, drawn-out wail. Always startling, along with the uneasy feeling that the peace which prevailed could not be taken for granted. In view of a war, a danger that was repeatedly evoked. And it was only ever a practice drill. Just in case. Are you against peace or something? It had been taken down some time in the nineties. And gone was the feeling of existing: here and now. Alive. Another week gone by.

The village had been divided. Those who remained occupied the core, the incomers had settled on the edge of the fields. That was where her house was too. It hardly merited the term. The money had only stretched to a cardboard box, which a bulldozer and a tractor had assembled in a few days from its individual components. Curious: first of all you spent your whole life waiting for a phone line. And then in three days you had a house. The walls were thin. Whenever anyone went downstairs, the basement shook. Still, they had a view of the fields. The façade was covered with ivy. Hiding place for a colony of sparrows. You only needed to clap your hands, and out they shot.

Was someone calling to her? Of course, Hans. He always knew when he had visitors. And for him, visitors meant anyone walking past his fence. He was just coming out of the greenhouse that he'd cobbled together from discarded wooden window frames. A tomato cutting in his hands. Shambling gait. As always, all the time in the world.

'Car not working?'

Sharp eye.

'Yes, that's right. The battery.'

He waved his hand. 'I know that one. I had one like that. But there were a few other things too. Write-off, they said. But it really didn't look like a write-off. Bastards. They just say it's a write-off. End of story. And it was a decent car, a real gem.'

On the harvested field behind his garden, the scattered bales of straw. Sagging electric wires under a broad sky. The last time he'd told her all that about his car was when Frau Thiele's son had been killed in a car crash. Seventeen. No driving licence. Two hundred things. You wouldn't wish that on a mother. But the kid hadn't been fit for anything.

She knew all his stories. That wasn't the issue. Talking to Hans once a day was a good deed. It allowed him to imagine that he still existed. It didn't bother him that she was only standing there because he was a poor sod. Being a poor sod was his capital. He chased her across the farmyard whenever he could. And this was his opportunity, the high point of his day.

'Did you know that wild bees are more industrious than

honey bees? Because they don't live in states, they live on their own. Or in loose communities.'

What did he mean by that?

'But all the bees are dying. I don't need to tell you what that means. If the bees die out, human beings have another four years.'

Always that conspiratorial outlook.

'Where did you get that one from?'

He held his head at an angle. 'I read the papers, I listen to the radio. Still: I'm not just lounging about.'

As if that were an achievement in itself. Although: in fact it was an achievement of a kind. What a gruelling effort it must have been. Staying alive without any kind of function. Pointless existence. At the expense of others. Only humans did that.

'I perceive the outside world through the medium of the media.' He held his hand to his ear and listened. Two external thermometers hung from his sitting-room window. He wanted to remain in control of the temperature at least. In the evening he went for a walk with his stripy ginger cat. Sometimes he said, Elisabeth and I . . . Elisabeth and he.

He had been married to a Ukrainian woman, who had headed for the hills long ago. For money that he had long ago squandered. He never mentioned her. He probably no longer even thought of her. Once he had walked through the village, drunk as a skunk, carrying an inflatable doll. No children. Animals met to mate, at least in passing. Temporary breeding communities. He had backed the wrong horse. He always did. But he couldn't stop. Why would he? Don't you want to invest? I mean, five thousand euros is nothing. Have a flutter! He just existed, sat in his mud hut, the only big house on this estate, a cave that looked more like a garage than a flat. A den with work benches and pictures he had painted himself. He was outside. For ever. Never again would he get a foot in the door.

Elisabeth came, rubbed herself against his calves and sat on his feet. She would have made an excellent dog.

'And I'm not doing anything stupid.' Omission as merit. How honourable. But that was enough. She wanted to go.

'Wait a second.'

He bent down, stroked the cat and picked something up.

A single rusty screw. He weighed it briefly, threw it in the air, caught it and opened his hand.

'Ah, you see, this is still usable.' He put it in the pocket of his battered jeans. He was satisfied. His day was saved. He had made a good catch, which he would drag back to his burrow, to all the other things that he might one day be able to use again. To his auxiliary store. An auxiliary life. Happy Hans. Poor sod.

'Enjoy the rest of your day, Hans.'

He had had his ration.

'I like it when you say my name. It feels good. Doesn't happen often.' He narrowed his eyes. 'You know, nobody talks to anybody. People just don't talk to each other any more.'

He meant himself, of course. He couldn't help it. Took the whole hand if you offered him a finger. Enough, now.

She left him standing there. He was used to it.

That weariness again. She would make herself some coffee. Wolfgang was still off with his ostriches. She had some time before he came home. Elisabeth was prowling through the garden. In the distance, the red and white blades of the wind turbines and the blinking radio tower.

The subject of the email consisted of two words. She suddenly felt her heart, that pulsating muscle, in her mouth: Just married. Even Inge Lohmark understood those words, even though she didn't speak English. Just, then. She clicked on the underlined string of letters. There was the photograph. A grinning couple, both in white. Two strangers. *Steven* it said. *Steven and Claudia*. Underneath, intersecting rings and two billing doves. Greeting-card birds. Harbingers of peace beneath a rainbow. Only some deviant kind of inbreeding had given them that innocent look.

She leaned back. On the table was the stack of lesson materials, on top the Year Nine seating plan. How untidy it looked. All those different handwritings. Hard to read. Some were barely decipherable. She would copy it out again. And down at the bottom edge. That was the place for the teacher's desk. She would have to write her own name there. Her eyelids were heavy now, her eyes were falling shut, but there were bits of lint swimming around on the screen, ceaselessly drifting away and reappearing. Her mouth dry, her throat very tight. Inge Lohmark felt as if she were choking on a boiled sweet.

Genetic Processes

The cranes were still there. In the field behind the house, where it fell away into a broad dip. They had been gathering there for weeks, grazing in the stubble fields and sleeping on their stilted legs in the ankle-deep water of the nearby kettle-holes. In the dawn a collection of grey dots, moving around here and there, and only gradually did the animals assume an outline against the dark landscape. A stalking troop that had got bigger by the day. Just birds that didn't know one another, an anonymous association bound together by a common goal: the coasts of Andalusia and North Africa. The rearguard of the western European migration towards the Mediterranean. The air was bitter and damp. There was already hoarfrost on the windowsill. It had never stayed here so long. Mid-November already. They looked uneasy, they seemed to be waiting for something. Was it migratory restlessness? Would they suddenly take off? Spread their frayed wings and rise into the air with trumpeting cries? To form an uneven phalanx with outstretched legs and necks. A crooked southbound arrow. It was still a mystery where they got their bearings from. The sun? The stars? Magnetic fields? Did they have an internal compass?

Inge Lohmark's breath rose like steam. It was cold. Definitely below zero. So what were they waiting for? How good

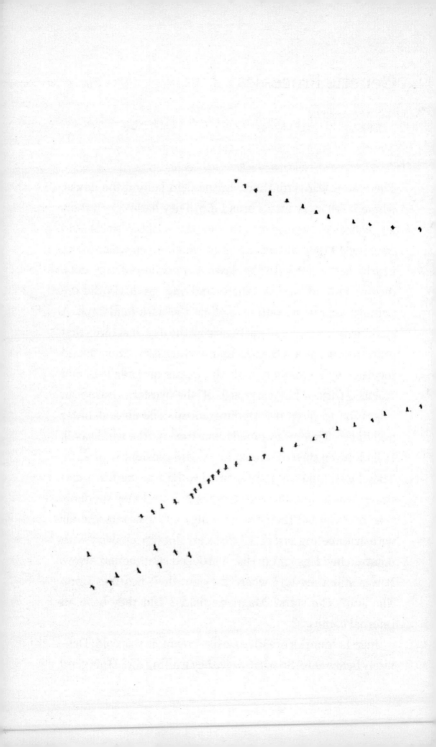

it must be to follow an instinct. Without sense or understanding. She closed the window.

As always, Wolfgang was already with his ostriches, leaving behind a half-laid breakfast table. A few crumbs revealed where he had taken his nourishment. There was a bundle on her chair. A crumpled pair of overalls, a vest, blue sports socks. His way of asking for his laundry to be done. It always had to be a pair of green overalls, because the birds' brains were too small to remember faces. They wouldn't recognise him a different colour. But you couldn't say that. He would never admit it. For Wolfgang they were the most intelligent animals in the world. He was practically in love with them. With their naturally painted lashes, with their sachaying gait. And because they were totally fixated on him. At least as long as he wore green overalls. Perfect example of false imprinting. It had gone so far that his hens wouldn't allow themselves to be covered if he was nearby. The breeding cock didn't like that at all. Every time, he puffed himself up and ran at him, hissing. The threatening gestures of the impregnator. A cock defending his territory was just as dangerous as a bull guarding his cows.

Wolfgang always thought it wouldn't work without him. Only because he had previously inseminated every cow by hand. A certain dominance heightened receptivity. And mating was a combat operation. In most vertebrate species, the sex act was accompanied by terrible noises. You only had to think of the pitiful cries of cats.

On one occasion Wolfgang hadn't been fast enough, and

the two cartilaginous toes of a running foot had hit him in the chest. It had even been in the papers.

Again he had stuffed the vegetable drawer in the fridge full of coconut-sized ostrich eggs. Who was going to eat them? The biggest animal cells in existence. An omelette for a whole school class. No wonder these animals actually lived in places where there were clans a hundred strong. But the two of them? They already had at least one too many. And you couldn't keep an egg like that. Shared mealtimes had become a rarity in any case. She ate her lunch at school with Aunt Anita, he in the little kitchen shed where he also prepared the food for the animals. Interested visitors often came by. And every few weeks someone from the *Ostsee* newspaper, to whom he would talk for hours about ostrich breeding. That the cocks' necks lost their redness after the mating season. That an ostrich made an accusatory trilling noise if it felt neglected. That young ostriches grew a centimetre a day. The importance of mixing the feed, even for the chicks, with little stones that helped them to crush the short grass cuttings in their robustly muscular stomachs. And that there were only a few restaurants in Berlin which paid good prices for ostrich meat. The thighs were most in demand. Supposedly the healthiest meat you could get. Lean and low in cholesterol. He always claimed it tasted like beef, but that would only occur to you because it too was dark. The visual trumps the gustatory. It was still in all the articles. Wolfgang Lohmark was the hero of the regional supplement. After all, he was one of those people who'd succeeded again. From being a former veterinary technician in the animal production sector to part-time farmer fattening up exotic animals that made for great photographs: stripy ostrich chicks under the infrared light. Ostriches trotting, ostriches doing courtship dances, ostriches in the snow. And the captions: *Giant Birds in the Steppes of Vorpommern. Feeling Broody on the Ostrich Farm. This Egg Would Feed Twenty-Five People. Aggressive Cock Attacks Ostrich Farmer.*

He had cut out and framed all the articles. They were hung up on the wall in his cellar. They had no business in the sitting-room. The ostriches weren't part of the family, after all.

As she brushed her teeth she looked at the cranes again. Even the last birds had left their damp sleeping places and were now shaking their plumage into shape, stretching their necks, testing the wind and the temperature. Now you could even make out the black legs on which they walked the field with a light and dignified stride. No comparison with the ostrich wobble. Here they were stilt-birds, beach-birds in their winter quarters. A double life. Another three days at the most and they would be off. It was a simple calculation. Any type of behaviour required a certain outlay of time and energy. And it was only worth it if the expected return exceeded the outlay. It was always a question of effectiveness. In everything. Where they were going was doubtless beautiful. The Mediterranean. What time was it, then? She would have to get going.

Marie Schlichter was standing at the bus stop. Head thrown back. Stuck up. High horse. The brain a windfall, ideally packaged in the shell of the skull. Doctor's daughter. Moved here to get some fresh air. But Marie Schlichter didn't take the air. Did she breathe at all? How irritable she looked. It was all conceit. Youth as life's incubation period. Waiting for the school bus. Waiting for her driving licence. Waiting to be able to move. The vain conviction that the best was yet to come. And she might be wrong there. But at least she kept her mouth shut.

The bus was on time and almost empty, as always. They all had their regular seats. Marie Schlichter at the front. Inge Lohmark in the second row back. The diesel engine was loudest there, and drowned out the noise that would be deafening in only a further five stops. She had thrown the whole seating arrangement into disarray. Driven Paul and his friends from the back row. Now the gang of thugs and late bloomers slouched in the middle zone. There had been curious glances, of course. They had all wondered why she was being chauffeured across the countryside in their bus every day. But there was much to be said for not driving yourself. Even just the risk of having an accident. All those idiots whose lives meant nothing to them. Not to mention the animals, all the deer and wild boar that stared into the headlights of approaching vehicles and refused to budge. The whole area was nothing but one big wild-animal rotation zone. Hunting stands all over the place. Clapboard sheds on tall stilts, reached by steep ladders. Tree houses for adults. And anyway, she'd always taken the bus. To school and to the regional capital. And in the autumn often with Wolfgang up to the north, to see the cranes. First by bus, then by train. Then by bus again. Endless hikes, bright autumnal leas. With Thermos and sandwiches. Until at last they came upon the meeting point of the colony, climbed into a hide and just sat side by side and studied the cranes. For hours. She had liked that about him. That they didn't have to talk. And he seemed to have been glad of it, too. His first wife had done nothing but chat; she hadn't been able to keep her trap shut all the livelong day. And Klaus, her previous partner, had wanted to talk all the time. Politics. About the government and the future. He got more and more furious as he talked, and she got more and more tired. And eventually she had a headache and Klaus was as red in the face as the men in the polyester suits with carnations in their buttonholes, when they stood on some stage or other beneath the banners proclaiming the future, talking about a world they'd dreamed up: one with efficient workers, fulfilled plans and improved means of production. *As we work today, so shall we live tomorrow.* You never knew if that was supposed to be a threat or a promise. Perhaps both. Eventually Klaus had taken the gloves off. But by that time they hadn't been together for ages. She was questioned anyway. For three and a half hours. She was familiar with that. Clean-shaven gentlemen. Elegant suits. Not those polyester ones. They just sat there nicely. She didn't need to incriminate herself. Other people had signed. And those few reports hadn't hurt anybody. And now it was being flogged to death. Even

Kattner had talked to her about it. And he wasn't exactly squeaky clean himself. For weeks he'd hauled all his colleagues into his office one by one, and no one was allowed to say anything afterwards. Hans said the Stasi had at least taken an interest in him before. When he felt particularly lonely, he read his files. Consoled himself with the knowledge of how important he had been in the past. At least to a few informers and their senior officer. What was in them? Hardly any furniture, hardly any visits from ladies. Just that he was anti-social. *In the residential property the other tenants considered H.G. to be a work-shy individual. The individual under investigation has no motor vehicle, but he does have a bicycle, which he uses almost daily. He is also very talkative.* Today you could do what you wanted. Except nobody was interested.

Jennifer got on the bus and pulled Kevin in behind her. To the back seats. After Paul's retreat it had become the testing ground for pubertal pairings. Jennifer had taken the initiative shortly after Kevin had come to school wearing a nose-ring. Gleaming metal in the middle of his face. The kind of thing you put on calves to keep them from suckling, and bulls to keep them attached to the staff. Going with each other was taken so literally. And Jennifer didn't need a staff. This little bull was tame.

Misted windows. Condensed water. Incredible heat. She wiped one of the windows clean. A dull sky over pale fields. Dun stalks of harvested maize in the ploughed muddy field. Earth sprinkled with green. A poorly sprouting catch-crop in favour of three-field crop rotation. Kale. Root crops after seed crops, turnips after grain. Churned-up holes in the ground after empty meadowland. Only a narrow, faintly glimmering strip of light hung above the pale blue forest in the distance.

Trees drifting past, the fissured branches of the bare linden trees. Glazed bus shelters. The panes misted by the nocturnal cold, stuck with scraps of poster, shattered by the young people of the village. Yellow posts, stop signs marked on tarmac passing-places and on overgrown kerbstones. And everywhere there were school-age children, alone or in small groups. They were collected like milk bottles. Milk bottles on the edge of the thoroughfare. They didn't even have school milk these days. No milk monitor to pay in the collected pfennigs every week. Vanilla, strawberry and normal: twenty; chocolate: twenty-five pfennigs. In winter, the lumps of ice in the milk crates. Kalkowski put them beside the radiators. It took till morning break for the milk to thaw. Calcium for childish bones. And fluoride for the teeth. Tablets in kindergarten. Today you would have the police on your backs if you gave the children tablets. The bus journey went on for ever. Three-quarters of an hour. It had nothing to do with all the bus stops, everything with the weird detours it took. The fundamental balance between effort and advantage didn't apply here. The bus turned into every cul-de-sac. Stopped everywhere. Everybody had to go along.

Even the horde of Year Fives and Year Sixes was nearly complete now. Why did they all come along too? Because they had no bus of their own. If they all died in an accident, they'd be able to close the regional schools as well. Then at least they'd have some peace and quiet. All that shouting. Lost their milk teeth, got huge great gobs on them. Keys dangling around their necks, mobile-phone cases and boxes for their braces. Their extra-large satchels took up whole seats. And they perched on the edge. With their shoes on the seats. But the pattern meant you couldn't see the dirt. The older ones, on the other hand, were like the living dead. Adolescent shuffling along the corridor. The rucksacks that would slip from slumped shoulders at any moment. Sleep in their eyes. Fringes that stopped just above where their noses began. Or no hair at all. Battle scars. And freezing red ears under baseball caps. Open boy-mouths. Teeth bared between grin and threat. Heads together. Lots of back and forth. Full on.

That uneasy girl in front of her. Thin, fine hair. A purple butterfly hairgrip that kept skipping over the seatback. Fur-lined hood. Fake fur. Was there such a thing as purple butterflies? In the rainforest, certainly. The variety of species was vast. An almost unbearable diversity. Strange fauna. After every expedition, always new species, sub-species and varieties. Bastards made fertile through isolation. No order there. Order had to be created. You couldn't get to the bottom of it. Television programmes at night. Patches of colour in the jungle. She had never in her life seen a king-fisher. Impossible business. In all those years. But she had seen a black stork, and twice an oriole. The yellow miracle bird. She was still small at the time. With her father. Now here came a girl waddling towards her. Tall, shapeless. And unkempt. Fat cheeks like buttocks. Fat breasts pushing their way through the fabric of her coat. Twelve at most. But everything already in place. Already been and gone. She stopped near the girl with the braces. Puffed herself up.

'You're to come to the front! To Juliane!' It was an order, not a piece of information. Juliane seemed to have her henchwomen under control. The butterfly set off at once.

The pecking order was formed to perfection. Kings and commoners. Worker bees stirring the nectar. In no other age group was the hierarchy so rigid. Rising through the ranks as good as impossible. Once an outsider, always a victim. And whippers-in could always be found. Hair pulling. Crushed rosehips down the collar. Lurking in wait on the way home. Stolen gym bags. Beatings in the bog. Wedgies. Food for the first-person-plural feeling. Someone was just putting Ellen in a headlock, too. It didn't look really dangerous. At any rate she was still fighting back. Let her fend for herself. It would soon sort itself out.

The bus stopped again. The latest entry was Saskia. As always she went straight to the back. Bent down to Jennifer. Three kisses on the cheek, but otherwise not a word. Her hair like a curtain. Rattling bracelets. A hand stretched out towards Kevin. Then she threw herself into the seat, put on her enormous headphones and turned the volume up a few more decibels. Sooner deaf than lonely. She'd briefly set her cap at Paul, to outrun Jennifer. But then the alternation between devotion and rejection became too much of a strain. Competition lost. Connection broken.

Silence on the back seat. Jennifer and Kevin were bored.

'Do you love me?' Jennifer's childish voice.

'Of course.' How grown up he sounded.

'Say my mobile number. You've got to know it by heart.' Feminine logic.

'Why? I've got it stored.'

'Come on, let's hear it.'

'Zero . . . one . . . erm . . . seven . . .'

'Go on.'

He didn't get any further. She helped him with the gaps. Then she probably let him kiss her. At any rate there was nothing more to be heard. But what did they have to talk about? There was nothing to say. People talked too much anyway. She and Wolfgang barely noticed that they didn't talk to each other any more because they didn't see each other for days at a time. What was the point of all that cuddling? People only stayed together because bringing up their young was so incredibly expensive. They could no longer rely on reinforced pair-bonding. The child had left the house. Mission accomplished. What else were they supposed to do? Write each other a greetings card? They'd got on well in the past. Now it was each to his own, and fine. He had work to do. They'd reached an agreement. They worked perfectly together. Eventually everything was finished. If she actually did take early retirement, he wouldn't just sit around. He'd once told her he liked second-rate women. Even before they were married. It had never been a great love affair. They hadn't needed that. She'd always liked the fact that he was good with animals. And what was love anyway? An apparently watertight alibi for unhealthy symbioses. Joachim and Astrid, for example. No children. It hadn't worked. And when it was too late for everything, each blamed the other. Walks together in pairs. Men in front, women behind. Joachim's bald head against Wolfgang's curly mane. Astrid's neurasthenic voice. Refereeing. Don't you think so too? No, she didn't. What did she care about other people's misery? They were pathetic, not pitiful. They beat each other half to death, stalked one another, and each threatened the other with suicide. Carnival at the arts centre. A band from Saxony. Four long-haired guys. Partner-swapping on the dance-floor. A lot of *Goldbrand*. Early-morning rows in the milk-bar on the marketplace. There was no doubt that they belonged together. An extremely effective mixture of symbiosis and parasitism. Siamese twins. If one of them died, the other would perish too. Eventually they'd moved away. To Berlin. For the culture. It had become impossible to watch anyway.

Now the bus turned into the cul-de-sac at whose end Erika stood, when she wasn't ill. In that case they would have taken that two-mile detour through the forest completely in vain. But Erika was well. At any rate she climbed on board, greeted everyone with her doggy eyes and sat down level with Frau Lohmark. The window reflected Erika, dimly lit. Against the pine wood, turned sideways. She had swapped her tight blue windcheater for an over-sized parka. Army green. The flag on the sleeve. No hammer, compass, sickle and sheaf of wheat. It still felt as if there was something missing. For the demonstrations back then she had just taken the emblem off. It was the same flag, after all. The parka couldn't be a hand-me-down from an older brother. She'd remembered a Langmuth. Maybe they'd been incomers after all. But not from the West. She was far too quiet for that. No one had turned up for parents' evening. Place of birth not mentioned in the class-book. Hardly any information. All under data protection. You knew too little about the children. And you spent more time with them than you did with your own husband. Let alone your own children. What was that she was taking out of her rucksack? Scientific tables. She flicked, looked for a particular page. Her birthday was in August. In the holidays. Leo. A shame, in fact. She could have paid a house visit. Viewed the children's room. A pin-board, felt-tip pens. Posters. Tadpole to frog. On house visits you knew straight away what was going on. As with this particular family. When she was still in teacher training. The mother had opened the door. Not in the first flush. Circles under her eyes and purple eye shadow. Baby in her arm and cigarette in her mouth. Talking to her about one of the six children who was in danger of being kept back a year. Every now and again a bit of ash fell on the baby. Then she blew on it quickly. Today you paid home visits only in exceptional cases. And Erika wasn't in danger of being kept back, and her behaviour wasn't attracting attention. Neither did she have bruises. Perhaps she didn't even have parents. She lived alone in the forest. She didn't even have a best friend. It always ended in betrayal anyway. Look at Saskia and Jennifer. A boyfriend? Out of the question. Menstruation aside. Pets, definitely. But not a dog or a cat. Small animals,

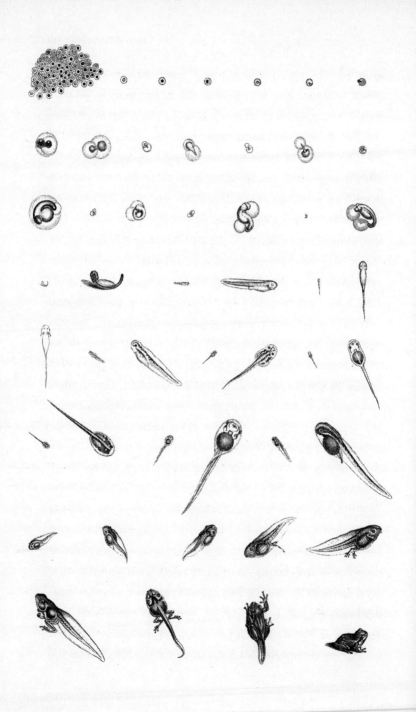

it would be. Salamanders, snails. Undemanding and easily looked after. A tree house in the garden. The fear of stroking a fawn. Staring into gleaming, oily puddles. Pulling the bark of birches. Striking flints together until they gave off sparks. Erika actually was strange. But judgements were delivered only at the end of the school year. Handwritten, in the old days, with computers now. An assessment. Between will and ability. It usually stopped with effort. No sign of the horizon of expectation. Don't stare like that. Eyes on stalks. Like sensitive feelers. Snail afternoons. As a child she herself had enjoyed playing with snails. Had built them an open-air house. Stuck branches in the earth. Gappy walls of thin twigs. Made little beds out of sand. And then she had laid the snails down to sleep. Even though it wasn't yet bedtime. Covered them up with scraps cut from cleaning cloths. The next day the snails had always disappeared. Gone walkabout. And then she'd gathered them up again. Taken them home. Sometimes there would be a snail among them that looked quite unlike the others. A visiting aunt. She had built a house for animals that carried their homes around with them. She had thought everyone needed a house. A bed. Even Erika. With a view of the forest. Got undressed. Just to be naked. Walked around the whole house. Her parents were away. Sat down on the sofa. It felt strange. Owl-cries in the night. Slugs. They were living creatures too. Just not pretty ones. For standing on. Perhaps she was stupid. Erika was still staring at the formulae. Say something to her. Anything. Just like that.

'So, are you doing lots of homework?'

Erika looked up, looked at her. Unsettled, of course.

'Yep.' Hesitant.

'Have you looked at everything very carefully?'

Erika was startled. So she was. What was this? What had she done? Not another word. Look away. Outside. Out of the window. Leaning out of the window. Pulse back to normal. What was up with her? Nothing at all. She hadn't said a thing. Hadn't given anything away. Drive on. Keep going. It was all quite normal. What was normal? Well, everything. The way snails mate. It went on for ever. The young ones climbed on top of the old ones. And their off-spring on top of the ones that had once been young. Young with old. They were all hermaphrodites. The division ran not between the sexes, but between young and old. What would the others think of her? Strange, it was almost calm. Calm before the storm. Or after the storm. No one was thinking anything. Jennifer and Kevin were dozing. Saskia had taken off her headphones and started grooming her mane. A journey. Every day. They were all still going to school. And Erika? Flicking through her biology exercise books. She wasn't stupid, anyway.

The sign on the way into town. They'd be there soon. Last night's dream. It was in Darwin's dining room. It was enormous. Everything made of glass. Flooded with light. Like the check-in area in an airport. But the teacher's desk was still there. All the seats were occupied. All by colleagues that she didn't know. So she went to the other desks, where the pupils were sitting, or the travellers, it was hard to tell. And only when she had sat down did she notice that Erika was there too, sitting opposite her. She looked properly grown up. Didn't seem to notice her. But under the table she pressed her knees against her legs. Very firmly. All the things you dream.

The class was sitting in the dark again. General state of gloom. Grey outlines against the blue glass window. Light on. The fluorescent tubes hummed. The front one on the left needed changing, as long as she needed it. Harsh laboratory light. End of the night-time calm. On their feet.

'Good morning.' Loud and powerful.

Faint echo in the choir. Narrowed eyes.

'Sit down.'

Textbooks and exercise books being shoved around, pens being rummaged for. It was a while before they were all in their seats and all their arms folded, as she had drummed into them.

'Books away.' How mild her voice sounded. That certainly wasn't her intention.

By now they were fully awake. Eyes wide. Sheer horror. Collective paralysis. They hadn't expected this. The usual sighing and whining and the inevitable doggy looks when she handed out the exercise sheet. Only Ellen and Jakob didn't say a word, accepted it all with no ifs or buts. Erika didn't so much as raise her eyes. Even Annika looked insecure, seeing her average in jeopardy. The whole programme. Only a week ago she had handed them back their last written exam. Form and function of the cell nucleus. The centre of all being. The one-way street from genetic information to protein. That was where the cell nucleus lay buried. The results hadn't even been too bad. Four fours, five threes, two twos, a one. But now came the freestyle event. They weren't here for fun, to pass the time. A performance was being demanded of them. As it was everywhere. An unannounced check was the closest the school had to offer. Preparation for reality, for the merciless sequence of surprising events. And it wasn't a good idea to announce the Abitur exams in advance either. It would make much more sense to launch a surprise attack. A big tombola for all the duffers. The prize: exercise sheets in sealed envelopes. Yes, in fact, the best thing of all would be to choose the candidates by lottery and take them out of class one by one throughout the whole school year. There wasn't really any skill in writing good essays after lengthy and tedious preparation. You needed to disturb the tried and tested pattern of alternation between the phases of communicating knowledge and checking it with little tests. Otherwise what you ended up with was Pavlov's dogs. And little bells don't ring in real life.

'This is the only way of finding out who's really been paying attention. On the way from short-term to long-term memory all kinds of things get lost.' That hadn't been necessary. They'd already surrendered. They brooded in terror over their sheets of paper and kept looking helplessly up. At her, and out into the black branches of the chestnut trees outside the window. But there were no solutions out there. It was all just theatre. Deep down they were happy to be challenged for once. All animals wanted to be dominated.

They were no exception. That was something. A glance into their impoverished existence. A paralysing but sublime feeling, and a day's ration of adrenalin. Thumping hearts in her hand. Yes, children, this was life. And life was rigidly divided. Into inner cause and outer appearance. Hard knowledge, dry bread. It was quite simple. The more you thought them capable of, the more they achieved. The desire for achievement was part of human nature. And there was no escaping nature's laws. Only competition kept us alive. No one had ever died from being overtaxed. Quite the contrary. Of boredom they had, though.

Another walk through the rows. From the cupboards to the window. The monstera needed watering again. Five dusty fingers that hung slackly down. An amazing thing. Apparently stubborn growth was another way of dealing with neglect. But we knew that. Probably even the most effective. It really seemed to be clinging to life. It grew and grew. Just kept going. But it wouldn't blossom in these latitudes. Soon the first snow would fall. Moderate climatic zone. Four regular seasons. Always sunshine, and rarely as much rain as there had been on the Californian coast. How good that had felt, back then. After her tour of the desert. The sky cloud-covered at last, the Pacific matt and grey. Brown pelicans plunged like kamikaze pilots into the sea. Young sandpipers ran along the drift line, chasing the waves with their long bills. Men patrolled the shore with metal detectors. Everyone in this country always seemed to be looking for something. And the palm trees didn't look like they did on television, all dry and rumpled. And here? There had been no sight of the sun for days. Everyone was talking about it. But they weren't plants. Claudia had said that when she pulled her lowered blinds back up. For years she had sat in the dark in the afternoon. Hidden away till adulthood. They weren't plants, but Claudia looked like a grub. A pale, thin-skinned ghost. Thin anyway. And that awful music. Smouldering joss sticks. Full notebooks. Diaries with little locks. Hidden keys. And dust everywhere. As if someone had died. That was even worse than the Christian teaching. Not a plant, but an animal. Mute and uneasy.

On through the rows. There had to be a check of some kind. A sigh somewhere. Tom sitting there again. A slumped sack. Laura pressing her torso against the edge of the table. Out of nerves or self-importance. Kevin, lying in wait. The nose-ring less than a hand's-breadth from the page, hesitant movements of the head. A cribbing manoeuvre. But Ferdinand was sitting far too far away. The gap between them exceeded any individual distance.

'Kevin, you can spare yourself the effort. Even I can't read Ferdinand's handwriting'.

Everyone turned towards him. The herd instinct. A small joke to lighten the mood. She wasn't a monster. He immediately stirred himself and looked intently at his sheet.

Where did the monstera come from, in fact? Was it perhaps a present? But who from? The days when teachers got presents were long gone. An armful of flowers on Teachers' Day. Twelfth of June. Height of the flowering season.

Whitsun roses in particular. The staffroom a great sea of flowers. Even prescribed gestures had their value.

And then again Jakob, the pampered, speccy creature. Ramrod posture. Look of a first communicant. He'd already skipped the first question. It wasn't arrogance, it was provocation. He really didn't care about anything. He'd given up on his life before it had even begun. Come to terms with everything, with unannounced checks and strict marking. It didn't matter a damn to him. Just like his father, a cosy man with a civil-rights beard and rimless glasses. Myopia wasn't the only dominant inheritance. Every parents' evening a demonstration. First rule of genetics: if the children were bad, their parents were even worse. The qualities that still slumbered in their offspring were fully formed in them. Tabea's hysterical mother. Single parent, of course. What had rattled her cage? For ever interrupting. That every child was a very particular individual, particularly hers. The things she came out with! The pitiful attempt to compensate for her own failed life with less wayward progeny. Grasping the nettle. The child was her investment. Genetic investment, all that was set aside for the future. It was the hope that one's own genes might prove advantageous in a new combination, and the success of that mixture might retrospectively distinguish the parent. Particularly when the other genetic carrier had headed for the hills.

You could actually smell the concentration. Sweat secretion. The attempt to bring forgotten matter back to light. Memory could be deceptive. Memory was deceptive.

Nothing but blind spots that filled the brain. Horror vacui. Nature abhorred a vacuum.

How innocently they frowned. How dazed. *Name four recessive physical characteristics and four dominant inherited illnesses!* They'd had it all. It was really simple. There were so many. On the fingers alone: polydactyly, brachydactyly, arachnodactyly. A question further on, there was even the family tree of a polydactylic family, illustrated by a black and white photograph. A father and his three children, stretching out their many vampire fingers, holding up the backs of their hands, gaze level, straight into the camera. From an old biology book. The thirties. A whiff of the chamber of horrors. Sideshow freaks. Strange hodgepodges. Crumpled creatures swimming in their own soup. Albinos, Hairy People, the Furry Girl, the Bearded Lady, the Woman without an Abdomen. The boy from her street when she was growing up. Humpy Reschke. He lived alone with his mother in a run-down half-timbered house. A hunchbacked manikin in wretched clothes. A burgundy silk shirt with frayed cuffs. Stretched over his hump. He lurched along the streets like a monkey. Neckless and bent, shoulders hunched. Perhaps it came from his hump. In his oversized hand a shopping net that dragged on the cobbles. His age was impossible to guess. Anything was possible. Normality was apparent only in its deviations. You needed the malformations to tell what was healthy. Monster derived from *monstrare*. It was all about visibility.

But what did biology books show today? Abstract pictures. Shiny, polished models of the introverted, twisting

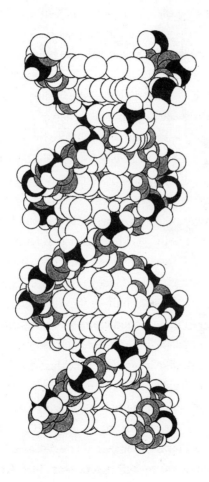

double helix. Scanning electron microscopes. A black and white group shot of the twenty-three pairs of sausage-shaped chromosomes of which everyone consisted. Wizened peas, monk Mendel with his thin glasses and his thick chain. Dolly, the stupid sheep. And an old pair of twins in blue tailcoats, displaying their sameness. Natural clones. Genetically identical offspring might be useful for research, but nature wasn't interested. Feeding the same genetic substance twice over? The point of that. And yet it was what the obstetrician had originally assumed, her belly was so huge. But if Claudia had had a twin sister, perhaps the twin would have stayed behind. And of course the fruit fly, the heraldic animal for all geneticists. There was always rotten fruit in the house. A model animal: *Drosophila melanogaster*. New generation every two weeks, huge number of offspring, only four chromosomes. And the hereditary characteristics were easily spotted. With a magnifying glass, when the creatures were anaesthetised. One day in the seminar there had been an Erlenmeyer flask on every desk, sealed with cotton wool. Inside them countless fruit flies in all kinds of mutations, for which some researchers had waited for years, or which they had helped along with X-rays: extraterrestrial eyes. Red or white. Patterned like a chessboard. Withered wings. Tiny chest hairs. She was supposed to anaesthetise the flies and sort them for their characteristics on a white sheet of paper. But if you used too much ether they died straight away. Too little and they woke up too early and flew off. The losses were great and ruined her results. Just dead and absconding experimental animals. Mendel had had it easier with his peas. Nature might speak through experiments. But every experiment has a life of its own.

In the section about inherited diseases there was only one single photograph. It showed a grinning mongoloid child with a butterfly on her hand. It looked like a cabbage white. Precisely. What was that all about? A pest and a freak. It used to be called trisomal idiocy. But you weren't allowed to say that any more. All the things you weren't allowed to say any more: Negros, Pakis, gypsies, dwarfs, cripples, retards. As if that helped anybody. Language was there to make clear what was meant. Invertebrates were called invertebrates, after all. There was always something you couldn't say. That the USSR was a multi-ethnic state. No, they were all just Soviet people. Recently they'd started saying there weren't even any different human races any more. You'd have to be blind to deny that one. If there were breeds of cattle, then there were human races. Even Mendel's laws were only rules today. It was all just syndromes, named after the people who discovered them. Like with islands. Flags hoisted in sick bodies. Immortality through diagnoses. Down, Marfan, Turner, Huntington. With no further reference to how dreadful it all was: idiocy, dwarfism, flat feet, infertility. Inherited St Vitus's dance. Early death. Life over at forty. As if it would be different otherwise. It applied to everybody. Every woman anyway. A third of your whole lifespan for nothing and nothing again. Post-reproductive survival. Another thing that only existed in humans. The genes wintered in our bodies and waited for better times. For the onset of disease, eventually. Carrying defects around. Genetics was dramatic.

Recessive succession was the most exciting bit. You had it, but it didn't manifest itself. Or perhaps it did. Eventually. A thriller. Open wounds. Non-clotting blood. Once she'd traced the family tree of the European royal houses. From Victoria down, almost into the present. Ramifying lines. A fantastic example of sexual and chromosomal inheritance. She had had to open the board up so they would all fit on it. The first carrier, her daughters and granddaughters. All perfectly healthy. But with a kick. Guilty mothers and their prematurely dead sons. Marked with red chalk. Half the boys bit the dust. Harmless falls. Minor car crashes. Slight injuries. Internal bleeding. Lack of supplies. The last tsarevich. A life on a silken thread. Even without a revolution.

Word got round about the picture on the board, and then she had to go and see Hagedorn, the headmistress. She was an agent of the class enemy. Imagine that! As if she'd publicly swung the Pomeranian flag. Okay, then: only Communists had fresh genes. But Hagedorn hadn't been able to do a thing to her. She gave them biological proof that the aristocracy had eradicated itself via inbred marriages. At the time she hadn't known that there were still kings and queens ruling somewhere in the world. Fairy-tale characters. Figures from Czech children's films. But the advanced loss of ancestors remained a fact. They could breed race horses, but not successors to the throne. It was genetic simple-mindedness. They'd only ever paid attention to blood, not to genetic inheritance. Humpy Reschke was supposed to come from a Catholic village where they'd kept themselves to themselves, before the war. Intensification of undesirable characteristics. Inbreeding depression always made its first appearance in the mouth. In the Habsburgs, a completely distorted jaw-line. Frayed beaks in ostriches. There still weren't enough breeding animals in the country. You never knew what you were going to get. Your only option was to mate animals of unknown origin. Blindman's buff. It wasn't breeding. Breeding only happened when you knew for certain which egg came from which parents. At least the cocks were still allowed to do the mating themselves. Even if Wolfgang was standing next to them. Natural mating. Every cock had two hens. A main and a secondary wife. They were always a trio. Ostriches lived in threes. The cocks sat on the eggs by day. It could all be so simple.

In front of her lay the family tree of the arachnodactylic family. Man and wife. Circles and squares, producing new circles and squares. Thin lines ramifying again. Only the born children counted.

Wolfgang had had two hens as well. A double breeding success. Two wives, three children. A square between two circles. Her and Ilona. And she had nothing to do with that woman. But you couldn't choose your relations. A triangle or a square. You couldn't even choose your children. Just give birth to them. Blood relationships didn't place you under any obligations. You couldn't depend on the kindness of genes. Not even on their selfishness. The prospect of

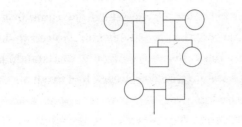

grandchildren wasn't looking great. A line into the void. A cul-de-sac. The dead end of a development. Claudia was already thirty-five. But ostriches never saw their chicks again, either. In the animal kingdom you can't drop by for coffee on Sunday. Gratitude couldn't be expected, and there were no returns either. No closeness. No sympathy. Not even similarity. The distribution of chromosomes in meiosis happened at random. You never knew what you were going to get. Most children didn't look like their parents, apart from one or two characteristics. The rest was deviation. The inheritance of eye colour was polygonal. And of hair colour, even more complicated. You couldn't predict any of it. You could only collate it in retrospect. Claudia got her brown, refractory, doggy hair from Wolf-gang and her bright-green eyes from his mother. Plainly she herself hadn't had any influence on the child at all. Claudia had once asked her if she was beautiful. What were you supposed to say to that? You look funny. Wide face, dark freckles, slight overbite. But funny was nice. A wrin-kled lump, ugly as afterbirth. Who had said that? Her mother. She was still mystified that that woman should have given birth to her. There was no real proof. Or had she said that to Claudia? Sometimes she had thought Claudia wasn't even her daughter. Although she had been there at her birth. After a thirty-six-hour labour. A day and a half. After twenty hours she'd stopped believing she was really going to have a child. Was convinced it was all in the head. A great swindle. An inflated belly and nothing behind it. Maybe a tumour, but not a child. A boy, everyone said,

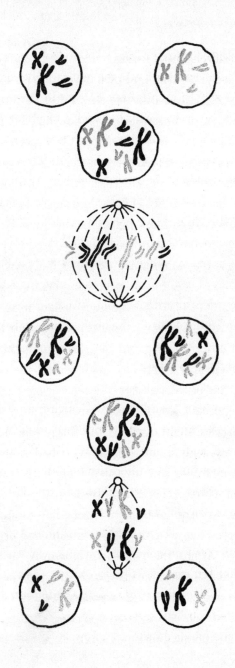

because her belly was so huge. She was two weeks overdue. Before they even let her into the maternity ward, the nurse put a red rubber hose up her bottom in the scrub room. Two toilets behind a partition. Black and white tiles, like in a butcher's shop. The cold water ran down her legs. There was no hot water. Apparently a blackout. Push hard, yelled the nurse, and held the pot a bit higher. Again and again. Push hard! She wanted to get rid of everything: the water, the shit, the child. Have her body to herself at long last. Three centimetres, someone said. And then: Not there yet. Time for oxytocin. When she thought it was about to get going again at last, no one was there. No nurses. No doctors. They were all with a woman two beds away, who had had an epileptic fit during the birth. Completely kicked off. And she was lying there on her own. Then the epileptic woman refused to accept her child.

How serious she looked. Erika. Attentive. Read her answers through again. Her eyes darting uneasily across the lines, her mouth spelling out individual words. She thought and added something. Even with her mouth open she was beautiful. The fluorescent lights flickered again. Went out. Ellen was sitting almost in the dark. Enough. The time was up anyway.

'Time to stop. The countdown's running.' Final spurt. Otherwise they would make everything even worse.

'Another ten seconds.' She knew that. At the end they always scribbled down some sort of nonsense. Just like that. So that they had something on paper.

'Pens and hands down.'

Groans again, but they obeyed. They all looked completely exhausted, as if they'd achieved something. Still, they were compliant. The best prerequisite if they were to be confronted with new material. She manhandled the big roll on to the stands. The black handle held the cards. Layered linen, washable and slightly cracked, but the chart was strikingly clear and beautiful. Nowhere were the Mendelian laws of classical genetics more simply and impressively demonstrated than here. The interbreeding diagram of two pedigree breeds of cattle. Dominant-recessive succession. A mixed bag. At the top, a black and white bull met a reddish-brown cow. What came out were two calves. But then, a generation later, the amazing regular division of characteristics occurred: sixteen, four times four possibilities. Pied bastards.

'The way characteristics disappear and reappear follows certain laws, and can be predictable. Write this down: As soon as two genetically pure individuals are crossed, differing in more than one characteristic, in the second daughter generation there is a real and lasting new combination of genetic endowment.' Everything was revealed in the second daughter generation. The throwback to the parental types. To the grandparents. Claudia's child would be more like her grandmother – like her – than she would be like Claudia herself. A triad. Three generations under one roof. That had been quite normal in the past. Her grandchildren might even have her blue eyes again. Pale, unpigmented. She didn't even know what eye colour that type was. Nothing had been discernible in

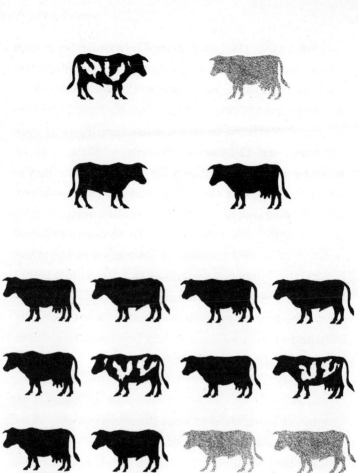

the photograph. The face distorted by a smile. Some man or other. Who spoke a different language. A foreigner. Her child wouldn't be coming home. Claudia wouldn't be building anything. Not on the polder meadows. Not in the Sauerland. Not in the smart suburbs of Berlin, where Frau Bernburg's son had moved. No point waiting. Nothing would be worth it. Counting your chickens before they're hatched. But what if she had a child. She'd got married, after all. A grandchild on a different continent. Twelve hours away by plane. She wouldn't be able to understand the child. She could only speak a few words. Hot potatoes in her mouth. Mickey Mouse English. Claudia had always made fun of her. Claudia got her urge to leave from Wolfgang. Whenever things got complicated he left the room. Once he'd actually walked out. Left Ilona and the children behind. For her. Hard to believe these days.

'Frau Lohmark?'

'Yes, Paul.'

'Why is it actually called a daughter generation?'

'What should it be called instead?'

'Well.' He fiddled around with his hood. 'Maybe something like son generation?' This was going to take a while. She got to her feet and leaned against her desk.

'Men's contribution to reproduction is tiny in the end. What are millions of semen cells compared with a big egg cell that ripens only once a month?' What was a quick act of sex in an elevated hide compared to nine and a half months' gestation?

'Every man is born from a woman. There are neither son

cells nor son generations. Reproduction is female.'

The girls giggled. They wanted more of this.

'Why, for example, do men have nipples? Even though they don't need to nurse?'

A blank.

'Erogenous zone?' Kevin. Of course.

'Because fundamentally embryogenesis favours femininity first and foremost. Even though it is clear from the moment of fertilisation what sex the embryo is going to be. The Y chromosome is only there so that development to femininity is suppressed. Men are non-women.'

All of a sudden they were listening. Now, at that precise moment, they understood one fact for the first time. Suddenly it all added up. At last they were eating the corn that she'd been scattering for weeks. If you put a bag over the ostriches' tiny heads, they allowed themselves to be calmly led around, and you could do whatever you liked with them. I can see something that you can't see. Now all you had to do was tighten the halter.

'Most hereditary illnesses are based on the X chromosome. That's why men have no compensatory factors. They are more susceptible, and they die earlier.' You might almost feel sorry for them. They really had some catching up to do. And that was why they had to come up with so many things: inventions and wars. Secret surveillance. Speeches in the playground. Renaming streets. Breeding ostriches.

A murder of crows crouched in the chestnut tree outside. They were jostling each other for the best seats. But none of them left the tree. They were intelligent. They could tell friends from enemies. Although the birds were forced to save weight in their brains to remain capable of flight. One crow didn't peck another one's eye out. Ostriches had small brains and still couldn't fly. Wolfgang didn't miss Claudia. He was used to not knowing anything about his children. His eldest had signed a document saying they wanted no further contact with him. He probably wouldn't have recognised his children in the street. And why would he? They had nothing to say to each other. It was the same with his brother. The son from his first marriage. The dead spit. And his gestures, his whole attitude. Rubbing his nose, bent over slightly. Men were different, in fact. They weren't bothered about their offspring. They had work and hobbies: computers, cars, parachute jumping, card-games, ostriches. Her father had always headed for the forest. Being a hunter. But her mother didn't feel like being a gatherer. It couldn't have continued like that for long. A simple woman. Cool. Perhaps she'd been attractive as a girl. But later on her beauty had been nothing but a robust declaration. She was nicely turned out at best. Even in hospital she had made sure she was always neat and tidy. Waxy face. An ice queen. Eyes like Bohemian glass. Artful, transparent, for no reason. Luckily she was dead.

'What's the name of the wild form of the cow again?'

A lonely hand. 'Yes, Ellen?'

'The aurochs.'

'Good.' Attention was already fading.

'And where does the aurochs live today?'

Vague unease.

'In Bavaria.' That was from Kevin. He seemed to think that was funny.

'The aurochs died out! Dead! Buried! For ever . . . Even before Steller's sea cow. Remember that!' Blood pressure. She had to sit down.

'Cattle are the oldest and most useful domesticated animals. They provide meat, labour and milk. In fact, it was with the domestication of cattle about ten thousand years ago that civilisation began. Civilised man has always depended on the teats of the domesticated cow.' Yes, that was a good image. She could have taught philosophy. The desktop covered with chalk. You couldn't get rid of it. However many times you washed your hands.

'Livestock rearing is a science in its own right. A form of breeding. Breeding for good. Selected characteristics are stressed. And bad ones suppressed. You choose the productive and companionable individuals and cross-breed them. Thus, for example, the East German Black-and-White dairy cow, which used to be very widespread around here, was crossed with red Danish Jersey bulls to increase the fat content of the milk. And their offspring were mated with Holstein cattle to increase dairy production. The goal was to create a new breed of cattle.' Towards the socialist cow. Long-living, fertile and robust. Three at a single stroke. Firm udder, strong muscles. A few years of fattening for dairy. And there it was, the perfect dual-purpose cow. The egg-laying wool-dairy pig.

'Culture comes from cultivation! From breeding and arable farming. Feel free to write that down. And pets, for example, are cultural artefacts. Living monuments. When individual breeds die out, they are lost for ever. It's not like houses, which you can build again if you find the plans somewhere.' She had always loved going to the Palace of the Republic. So bright. The light. Generous, really classy. White marble. Copper-toned glass. And that beautiful restaurant on the second floor. Upholstered wooden chairs at tables for four. The waiters all wore the same clothes, a proper uniform. Eventually they would build it again. But soon the cows of her childhood, the pied black dairy cattle, would be no more. The little bit of frozen sperm that they'd managed to find. The gene reserves were used up. It had been bred out.

'The dual-purpose cow is dead. Today there are only Holstein cattle in the fields. They are pure dairy producers. Real high-achieving cows.' Division of labour all over the place. Even the cows were specialised.

But the class had already lost their connection. They couldn't think two corners away. Not even one.

The usual hand.

'Yes, Annika.'

'Cows don't really mate any more, do they?' Her tone gave her away. It was a rhetorical question. She knew full well. She knew the answer and just wanted another gold star.

'Annika, cows don't mate anyway.' If the females mounted each other, it was only to show the bull how much in heat they were.

'So what should the question really be, Annika?'

A frown. Open mouth. So: she was embarrassed.

'Erm ... I mean cattle, of course. They aren't properly mated any more.'

'No.'

This was where it got really exciting.

'Natural mating is barely used these days. It's far too expensive to cart the bulls around. The cows are fertilised by the inseminator with frozen sperm.'

'Dirty breeder.' A thin voice from the back row. Ferdinand. Him too, then. Slow stroll down the aisle to the back, straight to him.

'Cow-fucker!' He couldn't help it. As soon as the gonads were functional, the urge to engage in sexual activity arose. And if it couldn't be enacted, it made its way verbally.

Back up the aisle to the blackboard.

'With the right arm up the cow's rectum, the operative feels around for the uterus, while the left hand in the vagina carefully pushes the sperm spray towards the mouth of the womb.' She imitated the gesture. A few suggestive arm movements. Fertilisation was a craft. And giving birth was work.

The girls repelled, the boys filled with disbelief.

That was real education. Not all that silly talk of foreplay and physical union. Snogging, stiff member, seminal fluid. Construction and function of the sexual organs, erogenous zones. Hygiene, illness, contraception. Sexuality was human behaviour, puberty a phase of its development. The bed the smallest cell of the community.

'And to get the sperm, the stock bull is led to the semen collection room. On a long staff fastened to a nose-ring.'

Kevin didn't bat an eyelid. Hats off. He was doing really well. Not so much as a flared nostril.

'In the semen collection room his mating partner is ready and waiting. A quiet creature that the bull mounts several times. Not a cow, but a bull.' It was far too danger-ous for cows. They would break their pelvis. The teaser bull didn't care. Stock bulls jumped on anything that looked remotely like a rear end. Even on a height-adjustable dummy on wheels.

'It only takes him two or three false mounts to be suffi-ciently stimulated and to unsheathe his penis. The semen collector takes it and introduces it into the artificial vagina.' Pre-heated rubber skin, correct temperature, optimal pres-sure, immediate ejaculation. They were excellent studs. And excellent earners. There were only a few high-quality sires. The rest ended up in the slaughterhouse.

'The sperm is diluted by a factor of a hundred, deep frozen and dispatched around the world. One ejaculation provides over one hundred inseminations. This is the effec-tive exploitation of a chain of release stimuli.' Sacral arch reflex. Tactile stimulation through false mounts, in which head and breastbone touch the back of the teaser animal. Climax the copulation reflex. 'It doesn't need feelings. It all happens automatically.'

Disillusioned faces. Yes, so much was uncontrollable. Apparently genuine emotions that were nothing but release stimuli. Whether it was a hiccup, the liquid that sometimes sprayed unexpectedly from your jaws when you yawned, or certain glands that were activated or weren't. Working machines. Hormonal variations. Chemical reactions. Preservation of the species. The birth process, nothing but the hormone-driven separation of mother and child.

'Are they gay, or what?' Paul. Grinning wasn't an expression.

'You're gay.' Kevin, of course.

The new teaching plan actually claimed that homosexuality was a variant form of sexual behaviour. As if sex life needed variants!

'The propagation of the human species knows only one way of passing on genetic information to the next generation. Remember the paramecia! What was it again? They can do both. Asexual transverse binary fission. And longitudinal fission, in which the single-cell organisms lie side by side and exchange tiny cell nuclei across a plasma bridge. You might say the paramecia invented sex. And what's the point of that? To refresh the genotype and correct possible errors. Recombination! Genetic diversity! That's the crucial advantage. Parthenogenesis and self-fertilisation are only any good for lower life forms. All halfway complex organisms reproduce sexually.'

Now she was actually able to turn the light off. It was bright enough, after all.

'The most important task of every organism is to produce the greatest possible number of surviving offspring. It's always a matter of passing on the genes.' From cell to cell, from generation to generation. The communication of information through threads of nucleic acid, macromolecules that ensured their continued existence at all costs, behavioural telegrams to the future world. Life wanted life. Even suicides regretted their actions at the last moment.

It was indeed amazing that every species produced its own kind. That cattle became cattle, and wheat wheat. And that from a grub-like foetus there developed a living creature which resembled its progenitors, regardless of whether they were ostriches, white-lipped garden snails or human beings. The species was a sexual community. The drive to reproduce was massive. Even tigers and lions were in its thrall, and sired infertile hybrids together.

'And from the anatomical differences of the sexes only one compulsive action is generated: the key has to go into the lock.' The rectum wasn't a sexual organ. The gay disease. It was really the most intelligent of all viruses. Its tactic was a work of genius. The immune system that was supposed to protect the body from infections. A thriller. Sleeping with the enemy. It was entirely logical: with sexuality, death too entered the world. Rolling condoms over broom handles: she had had to learn that specially for her lessons. Rubber over wood. By now she performed the exercise with technical precision. She herself had never used such a thing. And why would she have? Before, she had taken the pill. And eventually there had been no need even for that. All those hormones contaminating the water table and turning men womanly.

'And now please open your books: page one hundred and nineteen. Exercise twelve. Tom, read please.'

Annika snorted. The dray-horse was insulted.

'Decide which of the following character . . .'

What a stammer.

'. . . acteristics involve mu-ta-tions . . .'

Difficult word.

'. . . or modifications . . .'

Talk about reading ability.

'. . . and give your reason.'

And why was the textbook so informal with them?

'Thank you. Now it's everyone for himself. Answers in your exercise books, please.'

The freckles, animals' winter pelts, the muscles of a bodybuilder, Abyssinian guinea pigs. Mutations or modifications? Genetic programme or environmental influence? Inside or outside?

Enraptured squeaking.

'Oh look, guinea pigs.' That came from the heart. Those silly rodents always turned somebody's head. Laura this time.

Perversely located spine. Eccentric strands. Pointless breeds. Mutants. In no ecosystem in the world was a place reserved for such things. Claudia had got one for her twelfth birthday. A present from a friend. Nice friend. Blackmail, that was. Freddy. Supposedly a male. And then Freddy got fatter and fatter and finally gave birth to two babies. Identifying the sexes wasn't as easy with all mammals as it was with humans. But what could you expect from animals that looked exactly the same in both directions? Luckily the offspring were female. Those creatures were sexually mature at three weeks and knew no incest taboo. Freddy was beige with black spots. The standard finish. The little ones showed a few more of the characteristics of overbreeding. Furry body with pale blond strands. Dark blond rear with extensive bundles of hair like a train, with little lumps of droppings regularly caught in them. The stench. Pestilential bedroom. Luckily Freddy soon died of a brain tumour. They buried the remains behind the new block near the garages. They gave the little ones away.

Children and pets. It never ended well. Giving a child an animal was a particularly perfidious form of animal cruelty. Social-skills training, my eye. It was always a matter of life and death. The animal was delivered over entirely to childish omnipotence. And children weren't innocent. Much as one might wish them to be. Never had been. They were openly honest, openly brutal. Like nature. Sooner or later the animal died. Usually sooner. Escaped budgies. Hamsters flattened by powerful infant hands. Furry remains with rigor mortis. That was when the great cry went up. The toy had played its last. Grief looked different. Expired ornamental fish on the carpet. Flies' legs pulled out. Quartered frogs. It never made the papers. Although Rottweilers eating babies did. And it was perfectly natural. The hunting instinct. And what remained of nature, of the instincts? Tugging on the leash. Hoarse barking in the night.

As a child she had often spent her holidays with her grandparents. They had a field and a little patch of forest. Beneficiaries of land reform. White German Reichshuhn chickens pecked about in the farmyard. In the chicken house they perched on their bars in a strict pecking order.

In the stables a cow and a few pigs. Dead-looking sow in the straw. Under the infrared light the piglets fought their way to her teats, all crammed together. And there was always the risk that the fat mother would crush one of the little ones. Animals and children everywhere. Neighbours' children and grandchildren. Children and hay. Rolling in children. Smell of stables. Warmth of the nest. They stole the hens' eggs out of the straw and ate the potatoes that were meant for the pigs, straight from the steamer. Stuck their flat hands into the calves' mouths. Sucking reflex. Scared of the turkey. Its obscene wattle, those fleshy warts. As if it carried its sexual organs on its head. Two cats that were usually pregnant. Grandfather drowned the kittens in the rain barrel. With a stone in a bag. Late abortions. They didn't even have eyes yet.

'Which of you has a pet?' This was her opportunity. Animals were still a draw. Even after sexual maturity. But they had to have fur and teats.

Eight hands up.

She didn't even need to ask about snails. Dogs and cats. You saw straight away. Man had domesticated his worst enemy. Reduced the wolf to a doggy creature. From the forest to the basket. An undignified companion. And because its dribbling loyalty had become too boring, they had brought cats into the house as well. The idea that that even counted as domestication. Just because an animal ate from a bowl that had been put out for it. Purring was a feint. A provocation on the sofa cushion. Small wonder the tom-cat's penis had barbs.

Stubborn finger-clicking. That was what they figured. She'd have to keep this one short.

'Aha. Okay. Thank you.'

'And you, Erika?' She hadn't put her hand up. She hadn't said a word all class.

'My pet died. In the summer holidays.' Matter-of-fact tone. But her expression, that drooping eye. Out of touch with the times.

'Ah, I see.'

She hadn't wanted this.

Erika looked away, hunched her shoulders. A wounded animal. Asexual reproduction had one advantage. It left no corpses behind. Paramecia were potentially immortal. Once she'd been allowed to choose a kitten. A black one with orange patches. It had been the prettiest one, but not the strongest. A week later it was dead.

Time to change the subject.

'Don't forget. There are genetic dispositions and environmental influences. The genotype is unalterable, but the phenotype can turn out in very different ways according to living conditions. The appearance of an organism isn't determined entirely by its genetic inheritance. DNA provides only preconditions.' Genetically identical beans that flourish to different degrees in different soils.

A hand up.

'Yes, Tabea.'

'It's like horoscopes. It depends what you do with them.' Okay, money from the stars. Not just stupid, but cheeky, too. She really was a moonchild.

She turned away, to the window. The crows had disappeared.

'Not every thought deserves to be articulated.' Now turn around.

'Tabea, if you want to stay at the Gymnasium, please check in future whether you really have something substantial to contribute to the lesson.'

Right in her face.

'And before you open your mouth.'

She was still thunderstruck.

'And find out your blood group. And your parents'. Including rhesus factor.'

Bell for break.

'Off you go, to your next class.'

See which of the children had lost a father. She was on the right side. It was all in the teaching plan. And more realistic than the exercise in the book with the babies switched in the obstetrics ward. And practical experience was always called for. Now there were certain compelling parent-child relationships. The truth was reasonable. Even to children. Especially to children, as early as possible. Frau Bernburg had once rubbed her nose in the fact that her lovely son wasn't her husband's. Cuckoo in the nest. Carrying a seedling around inside you for nine months could make you very confident. And powerful. It wasn't only reproduction that was female; staying a step ahead was female too. Frau Bernburg's son wasn't all that lovely, either. More a souvenir of a lovely time. There had been problems with a second child, too. They had told her that straight away. Claudia was rhesus positive. She was rhesus negative. Formation of antibodies. One child had been enough for them. Every little helps. Wolfgang's words. She didn't need a reminder like Frau Bernburg.

'You may go.'

They all dashed out. And Erika? What was she waiting for? She walked very slowly past the teacher's desk. As if she was doing it on purpose.

Steady gaze. Her green eyes.

'Thank you.' Very quietly.

'You're welcome.' She was sure she wouldn't tell anybody.

Thiele was sitting in the staffroom. All on his own.

'No lessons?'

He raised his hand. It looked as if he was dismissing her.

'Nope, free period. Year Twelve have their first careers advice classes today.'

What would they be doing? Probably a visit to the job centre. Learn to fill in forms for unemployment benefit. She threw the stack of tests down on the seat next to him. On the top was Erika's sheet. Her boyish handwriting. Big and angular. Hardly any curves or loops. She'd actually got almost everything right. She would save that one for last. The next sheet. Jakob. Where was her red pen? Thiele could drive you mad. The newspaper was in front of him. But he drummed on his lunch box and stared into the distance.

'So: what did you have last?' He didn't know what to do with himself. An animal exposed. Pitiful.

'Year Nine biology.'

'Mhm.' A nod. He looked dreadful. Kattner had taken his office away even before the autumn holidays. Apparently they were doing some sort of conversion. Probably more of a resettlement. Anyway, he'd been flexing his muscles lately. He'd wanted to stop her writing up the names of the losers on the board. But who else was supposed to put the mats and equipment away after the lesson?

'Well I had Year Eleven. Yep, Year Eleven's what I had. Latest news. Social studies, almost. You know, this isn't really even history. History has to be put together in an orderly fashion. It was all only yesterday . . .'

Jakob was already ten marks down out of thirty. And she was only on the third question.

'And you?'

Now he shifted closer, took a sheet from the pile and inspected it.

'Ah, genetics . . . Mendel and so on.' He seemed to have something on his mind.

'You know what's crazy, Inge?' He set the paper back down again. 'I didn't do genetics in school! Just Michurin and Lysenko.'

'Ah.' The garden god and the barefoot professor. Sprout mutations and wheat from Odessa.

The door opened. Meinhard came in. He nodded and sat down silently. Amazing, given his bulk. Thiele spread the newspaper out. She wrote the mark under the last answer. First one done. Next candidate. Tom, stupid as a sliced loaf. If she hurried, she'd have finished marking by morning break.

Thiele started giggling. 'Michurin established that jam contains fat.'

She knew that too.

'That's why we have it with everything. Jam in pails.' Both of them, in chorus. Another reflex. 'Frère Jacques' for the young pioneers. Children's campfire songs. Four-fruit jam out of little cardboard pails. And rosehip tea from buckets. Learning from the Soviet Union means learning to win. That marked a person for life.

'We had everything. School gardens and a Michurin Circle. Even an agronomists' club.' He stretched his bony hands across the table top.

'Michurin, never heard of him. Who was he?' Meinhard was finally coming out of his shell.

'Michurin bred hundreds of new varieties of fruit. Frost resistant and product yielding.'

Sometimes even tasty. Winter butter pear. Pound-and-a-half Antonówka.

'Yes, he just crossed everything with everything.' Thiele, very enthusiastic. 'Strawberries with raspberries, almond and peach. Even pumpkins with melons. Love matches between different plant varieties! That was what they called it.'

Love matches, my eye. Organisms forced to breed together. Forced marriage is what it was. Fruit with vegetables. It was practically immoral.

'Do you know how he died?' Thiele grinned in anticipation.

Old joke. 'I know. Falling from one of his strawberry plants.'

'Exactly!' Thiele's hoarse laughter. Smoker's cough. His torso quivered.

Meinhard still didn't look impressed.

She set the red pen down.

'Michurin's great achievement lay in finding the ideal match for every agricultural crop.' Sprout mutations. Mixing saps. A form of grafting. The principle was even popular in schools. You sat an idiot down next to a swot and hoped the swot would exert a positive influence. Teacher as gardener. Hoeing weeds and hoping for harvest. One day. Except unfortunately the heads of the clever pupils didn't grow on the bodies of the stupid ones. Grafting was pointless there. And whose head was it supposed to be? She didn't just want a classroom full of Annikas. Growing a tree from a cherry stone took for ever. And the more branches you grew, the lower the yield. The Martens children had quite small heads, too.

Meinhard unpacked his breaktime snack, as if he knew now. When in fact he hadn't a clue.

She hadn't finished yet. 'In those days people thought you could change plants by having a perfect knowledge of their living conditions. So they studied the needs of cabbages, potatoes and wheat. All just so that they could make new demands on their environment. But only the most desirable demands, of course.' A single process of accommodation and reaction. The education of pulses. The conquest of bread. The land as a laboratory. Experiments for which plants were castrated to prevent them from fertilising themselves. An army of farmers armed with tweezers and brushes took to the field to remove anthers and artificially pollinate plants. Bee people.

'Worked, too.' Thiele, being superior. 'Jarowisation.'

So long since she'd heard that word.

'The summerisation of wheat.'

Stimulating the germination of the grain even before it was sowed. Seeds lit around the clock with ultraviolet light, steeped in barrels. Huge warehouses. Open windows in below-zero temperatures.

Meinhard chewed and nodded, but still didn't look as if he'd understood. How could he have done? He'd grown up without a collective, he had never known harvesting assignments or potato-picking holidays. He'd probably never even worked in a field. He hadn't the faintest idea what they were talking about.

'To put it crudely: they thought that wheatgerm, if it was first put in the fridge, could also be planted in Siberia.'

'I get it.'

Could have fooled me.

'Of course it didn't quite work. And if something did work from time to time, the effort far exceeded the rewards.'

'That's not true.' Thiele, in fighting mood.

'Oh, come on. Lysenko was beating his head against a brick wall. Talk about creative Darwinism. It was pure kolkhoz biology. Natural laws didn't apply. The practice was enhanced and basic theoretical knowledge ignored. Theory was secondary.'

'But the theory worked!' Thiele was quite serious.

'But only theoretically.'

'And how else would you expect?' He was losing his temper.

'Let's see. The theory of gravity is only a theory.' Now Meinhard was playing the arbitrator.

'True words, my friend.' Praise from the elder. Thiele the Wise.

That was what they'd come to believe. Such nonsense. 'Yes, but obviously the planets stick to it. There's no theory without practice.'

'No, there is. It's like in maths. There are some things you don't know what they're for, just that they're factually correct. That they're internally coherent.'

As if that meant anything. Every individual human being was internally coherent. It was a pure instinct for self-preservation.

'You can always rely on maths. It's a clean science. The most dependable of them all.'

My goodness! An eager beaver! Fresh out of their studies, they were still believers.

'And so easy to correct.' She couldn't hold her tongue. Anyway, numbers were easier to decipher than Ferdinand's scribbles here.

Look at that. Meinhard even knew how to frown.

'At least there's no faking in maths, it was . . .'

'Lysenko wasn't a faker!' Thiele was furious now. 'He mightn't have had much of a clue, but he did have a vision. Grain in the Arctic Circle! Rebuilding of nature! Bread for the world! You mustn't forget: we were the first people in space. We were ahead of the game.'

Thiele's subject. Ultraviolet radiation and space travel. Socialist sister country. To the sun, to the moon, and to Siberian wheatfields, sugar beet in Central Asia, strawberries in the Steppes. From the kolkhoz to the cell. Follow me along the Michurin Way. Which leads precisely nowhere. Wheat with multiple ears on a single stalk. Of course: if summer durum wheat could be turned into winter durum wheat, then why not wheat into rye and spruce into pines? 'It's all well and good. But did there have to be so much nonsense? All the things they announced: that bacteria can be turned into viruses. And plant into animal cells. Or that cells can be formed from dead organic matter, and blood vessels from egg-yolk. What about square cluster planting of potatoes, and pig huts? And open cattle stalls? They were supposed to be a natural way of keeping livestock. Don't make me laugh! The cattle stood around in their own shit and caught their death in the winter. Proletarian biology might have claimed to be practically oriented, but it was completely unusable.' If you cut animals' tails off, it didn't mean you'd get tailless offspring. Experiments took time. Conclusions took time. Everything took time. But nobody had any time. They wanted quick results. Big harvests. Bread on the table. Fat ears of wheat and fat udders. Little Jersey bulls with fat Kostroma cows. They wanted to make sweeties out of shit.

Thiele sighed. 'As a matter of fact, the most important method of Marxism-Leninism consists of enquiring into things.'

'Really? I wouldn't have thought that.' Meinhard was a

curious character. No beard to speak of. But hair in his ears. If roebuck are castrated too late, they grow a wig instead of antlers.

'You're right, Inge. A bit too much propaganda. We didn't need that at all.'

First the Colorado beetles, which American planes were supposed to have dropped on them to destroy the harvest. One pfennig each. Jam-jars full. And the maize that was suddenly being planted everywhere, and contaminating the ground with nitrogen? Sausage on a stalk. Such nonsense. Nobody had ever seen wheat with multiple ears on a single stalk. The Michurin fields stayed barren. Dried-out fields in scorching summer heat. In the end it was the sparrows that ate all the seeds. And what did they learn from that? That the sparrow was an economic pest of the first order. And: the yield of the harvest essentially depended on the correct seeds. If an experiment isn't going to work, you have to try and force it to say the right thing. Words of her old genetics professor, when he discovered her dead fruit flies. Everyone had known what he meant. Say it with flowers. The bare facts. Little push in the right direction. Make the whole thing add up. Anything that doesn't fit must be made to fit. After the theory of everything, the gagging order. 'In Budapest they even destroyed whole fruit fly cultures. As a symbol of Morganism.'

'All right, Frau Lohmark. Your American capitalist genetics has ended up victorious too.'

It wasn't her genetics. There were clearly still different persuasions even in biology.

Thiele was sulking. He folded his arms. He always had to take everything so personally.

Meinhard rested his elbows on the table. 'What I don't understand is: what's so capitalist about genetics?'

A glance at Thiele. This was one for him.

'Well. Saying everything's an investment . . .'

Thiele waved his bunch of keys in his hand.

'. . . and that life is preordained. Fate: poor stays poor, rich rich. All that bourgeois shit.'

Still coming out with the old slogans.

'The redesign of society doesn't stop at nature. Nature is a part of society! It needs to be revolutionised too! And if we change our environment, our habits, then sooner or later we change people as well. Being determines consciousness! That much is clear.'

The keys fell on the table top.

'I mean, something like intraspecies competition . . . that can only be asserted in a society in which it is daily applied. It isn't a natural law, it's a construct of the capitalist world view!' He was actually blossoming. His ears were bright red.

'Oh, Thiele, we've lied to each other about this one. Denied that there are such and such kinds of people. Good and bad, lazy and hard-working. You can't just turn any old peasant child into a university professor. Upbringing isn't everything. Talk about biopsychological unity. We tried extremely hard with the last lot of students. All-nighters through the summer holidays. Unpaid extra tutoring. But the victory of socialism is by no means as certain as the law of gravity.'

Thiele leaned forward. 'But it has often worked. What about that marine biologist? She came from a family like the Martenses.'

'Not quite as many children. But more alcohol.' Exception that proves the rule.

'And besides . . .' Thiele got up now, pushed his chair back '. . . if we only taught things that were absolutely watertight, we could close down all the schools.'

'But maths . . .' Meinhard again.

Thiele dismissed him with a wave. 'Don't worry. You'll learn that there are more important things in life than your stupid equations. Because I can tell you one thing: reality, events in the world are incalculable. Then a bomb goes off suddenly, and before you know it it's the next world war.'

He supported himself with both hands on the arms of the chair. He looked as if he was about to deliver a speech. Above their heads. 'We were concerned with overcoming existing conditions, with overcoming the capitalist form of society.'

'But nature can't be overcome.' That he couldn't see it. He was slowly starting to get on her nerves. Wisdom in spades. The older the bulls got, the more eccentric they became.

Meinhard groaned. 'God, you're still stuck in it.'

'Tell me, how long have you been here?' Thiele sat down again. Listening posture.

'A year and a half.' Quite proud. As if this was Siberia.

'And? How do you like it in the Zone?'

He'd never asked that before. Why was he so interested in it all of a sudden?

Meinhard hesitated. He was probably suspicious. No wonder.

'Oh, I don't know. Well. Very well, I mean. It's not done yet.'

'You see!' Thiele raised his forefinger. An old school-master. 'Because this is a utopian country.'

When Communists dream. Wild-East fantasies. Now he was really getting on his high horse. Wealth for all. Seaweed on bread. The brotherhood of all nations. Melting the polar ice caps, watering the deserts, taming the bears. Drying the Mediterranean Sea. Getting rid of cancer, old age, death. Still, it was more original than organising private space flights or cloning sheep. They'd created a hybrid-embryo that spring. A mixture of cow and human that they had destroyed again after three days and five cell divisions. Superman was only a matter of time. Soon they'd really graft the heads of the intelligent on to the bodies of the stupid. 'You're already talking like Kattner.'

'Oh, him. I'm telling you: Kattner's going to finish us all off. One by one. In the end he'll be teaching all by himself.'

Conspiratorial expression.

'I'm going to stay here anyway! Until the water rots in the pipes.'

He folded his newspaper.

'And one more thing; this, here. It's a little step back. But coming generations will prove us right. Future history. A bit of grass just needs to grow over it, and then we'll have another go. A real revolution.' He leaned back. 'You can't work with these textbooks. The end of Communism is being sold as a revolution. It's incomprehensible. Everything's going to the bad.'

'Same old story.' It was true.

Thiele got up again.

'Inge, we had no reason back then! There was something at stake in those days. But this . . . Calling an annexation a peaceful revolution – a revolution! Just imagine.' His voice was nearly breaking now. 'Don't make me laugh. Bloodless though it was! You need violence to get anything moving. No one today has an inkling what it means: fighting. For a country. For the right cause. Heads have to roll. Barricades burn.' He was at the door already. 'All those attacks on revolution. It's a falsification of history!' Unimprovable. Last words. The door slammed. Where was he going to go? Breaktime wasn't for ages.

They were all standing to attention in the playground. The whole school population, arranged by year. On the left the upper classes, on the right the lower. They all fitted side by side, along the edge of the brittle pavement slabs. At least if they were organised by size. The teachers next to the class representatives. As expected, Annika had won the election. She stood there, ready for battle. Her back was tense. Still, it was a posture of sorts. She would have made a good secretary for the Free German Youth Movement. All they needed was for them all to hold hands, like in those gormless human chains they'd made back then, along the B 96. A big cross through the two German nations. Strange. She no longer had any idea what it had all been for. Or against. Long-term damage from attending all those mass demonstrations. Eventually it was only the type of flower that told you whether it was May Day, the Birthday of the Republic or Teachers' Day. Lilac, dahlias or Whitsun roses.

Then here came the master of ceremonies. Kattner stepped out of the classroom block, hurried with long strides down the corridor of pupils and teachers and stood on the top step by the main entrance.

From his briefcase he took a pistol, the size of a ladies' revolver, and pointed it into the sky. That was the sign to keep your head down. Kattner's address to his people. Every first Wednesday in morning break.

In fact he wanted a little brass band to play a fanfare every time, but they'd dissuaded him from doing that. That was all they needed. With trumpets and trombones. At the end he had been quite keen on their idea of starting his Wednesday sermon with a shot from the pistol that they didn't need again until sports day in the summer. The bang. A starting shot.

'Dear pupils . . .' Artificial pause. 'And dear colleagues.'

Always those exaggerations. His salesman's grin. Cattle didn't have facial expressions. They could only communicate with their bodies.

'School is – this is in its nature – a place of change, of alteration . . .'

So, a flag ceremony. Except without the flags. But with lots of ceremony. Let a hundred flowers blossom, let a hundred schools compete with one another.

'Here you learn to master foreign languages . . .'

If she narrowed her eyes, Kattner's head was just a pale dot against the glass doors. Everything looked exactly like the school entrance on the old twenty-mark notes, those little green rags. Showing children coming out of school, staggering cheerfully into the afternoon. With short trousers, lunch boxes and satchels that seemed to have grown out of their backs. The few steps to the glass doors. A flight of steps for class photographs. Claudia's first day. The gap in her teeth, above the bag of sweets she clutched. Right at the back. Third row. Tall. She'd rather have had a son. Sometimes she dreamed about a little boy. About ten years old, with sad eyes. Burying his face in her lap. Like a puppy. Smelling of fir trees and sea wind.

'. . . Here you learn the encounter of traditional culture and history.'

Where had he copied all this from? Was anyone actually listening? Meinhard's moon face. A button on his trench coat was open. He looked like an old matron. And Thiele stood there, head hanging, as if at a funeral. The pupils were amazingly calm, better behaved than ever.

Then Frau Bernburg came marching in with Year Twelve. They took up their position. Each one with a green book under their arm.

Kattner took no notice and just went on talking.

'. . . Here you become familiar with the fundaments of science.'

What was that smell? The windows to the toilets were closed. It stank of vomit. Butyric acid. Had someone thrown up in the playground? Alcoholic poisoning. Down the nose.

'The humanist Gymnasium is an achievement of our free democratic constitution.'

Humanism had once been a term of abuse.

Behind him a big white patch on the wall. The result of covering up the graffiti. The main thing was that the façade looked right. And he was the one responsible for slogans.

'Because it is only in our free, democratic society that the knowledge can be communicated which . . .'

So it was the same thing all over again. Take democratic and free and substitute it for socialist. And what emerged was always the formation of well-rounded personalities. And humanity was always supposedly at the centre.

In the old days, the children were supposed to be brought up to be progressive, peace-loving people; now they were to be free. And freedom was nothing but an insight into necessity. No one was free. And no one was supposed to be. Even compulsory schooling was nothing but a state-organised deprivation of freedom. Concocted by the education minister's conference. It wasn't about communicating knowledge, it was about getting the children used to a regular day and the dominant ideology of the moment. That meant an assurance of dominance. A few years of supervision to prevent the worst. Gymnasium as a way of keeping them quiet until they reached maturity. Good citizens. Obedient underlings. A constant supply for the pension system.

'. . . Analysis. Interpretation. Independent activity. A capacity for judgement. Critical thinking . . .'

She was familiar with that one. Critical thinking was always allowed. Except that it had to follow the line. In a sick system more than anywhere, you had to pay attention to your health. And the core of all health was conformity.

'. . . but creativity above all!'

Now there was still the killer argument. Creativity was like God. Couldn't be measured, couldn't be proved, hence non-existent. A figment clung to by failures. Anyone who couldn't do anything was creative. And the startling thing was that Frau Schwanneke was blissful. As if he had awarded her a decoration in front of the assembled crew.

'The division of all knowledge into individual, independent disciplines is only makeshift. All subjects are ultimately interrelated.'

So? What did that mean? All human beings were interrelated. When you were born you toppled straight into the trap that none could escape. They were all creatures that had fathers and mothers. Two people at whose mercy you were for years and years. Dependence created through long-lasting deprivation of freedom. Silence during the lunchtime nap under Dürer's hare. His long beard-hairs, the cross of the window frame in his black pupil. Paws together, ready to jump. Eventually habit kicked in, easily mistaken for closeness. The repulsive skin on the hot milk. Stockholm syndrome. And all they left you with was genetic material.

'We are never done with learning . . . we live throughout our lives . . . not for school, for life . . .' It would have made a perfectly good motto on a calendar. Now all that was missing was learning, learning and learning again. The stench wasn't going away. Best to breathe through your mouth.

'. . . we go to school throughout our lives.'

And they did. But what good did it do? You couldn't prepare yourself for the greatest challenges. Being born, growing up, having a metabolism, ageing. You couldn't learn that. It happened all by itself. It was still a mystery to her why her parents had been together. Two people who slept in the same double bed at night for unfathomable reasons. Without compulsion. Anyway they weren't a couple. Never had been. And had never become one. Father had died so young. Just keeled over, as if he hadn't had the courage to fail to come back from a long walk in the woods. She had often been out and about with him. Studying animals and collecting mushrooms that her mother reluctantly cooked for them. And every feather they found, they stuffed into a bag that they emptied out on the meadow in the spring. As support for the swallows when they built their nest. Once they'd had the opportunity to be there. Hammered clubs against the tree trunks in the army of beaters. Chased the wild boar into the path of the shotguns. In the undergrowth the rifles of the ones with the hunting permits, the Party members, his colleagues. A privilege of his office. Local Party leadership. Not even her mother knew what he really did for a living.

'We live in a knowledge-based society, education is the highest good . . .'

The idea that money should always be invested in education. Anyone who studied left anyway. The educational drive was fathering, feeding and reproduction. Praise of monogamy. The dilemma of the preservation of the species. Cells that multiplied and then died away. Lumps of protoplasm. Tiny chambers, microscopic units, greatly enlarged. *Omnis cellula a cellula.* From individual parts a whole. High-level division of labour. Every organism an extraordinarily complicated machine. A state in which even the smallest part has its task. Colonies of genetically identical components. The coexistence of cells at the expense of others. The better state. The more beautiful country. Our homeland. The sun rises in the East. Father's words. Towards the light. Like a plant.

'. . . We are making this school fit for the future . . .'

Once she was allowed to cross the border with him. To his birthplace. New transport network, functional residential blocks, the market like a crater. He didn't recognise anything. On the station, the name, translated into Polish. Amazing, in fact. Just because the same geographical position was still inhabited. You had to rename towns when the urban genetic material changed too much. It wasn't the same town any more. A whole new species.

'. . . And only together . . .'

Cooperation with the state powers. Mutual aid in the animal and the human realm. Cooperative behaviour was answered with cooperation. As you do to me. So do I to you.

Sometimes coyote and badger came together to hunt gophers. The badger dug the holes to entice the gophers from their lairs. In the end the coyote struck. When eating, it often gave the badger priority. But sometimes it ate the badger. Collaboration was always a risk.

'. . . And only together, with one another and . . .'

A giving and taking. Was that what Kattner meant? In the old days the chickens got the cow-dung and the cattle the chicken litter. Protein for biomass. Undigested energies, fallow talents.

'. . . Development doesn't only have to do with growth . . .'

Cell renewal at any cost. Service according to regulations. Smooth sequence. The cell was political. The family the smallest cell of society. The population pyramid. At the top stood the family. Which family? She had a husband who loved ostriches, and a daughter she could barely remember. The cell, the site of all illnesses, of all evil. Father dying like that. Her hair had turned white. In just a few weeks. Sudden withdrawal of melanin. She had just turned thirty. Claudia at holiday camp. How shocked she had been when she came back. Her child barely recognised her.

'Quite the contrary: we are shrinking. But we are shrinking healthily . . .'

That stench was really appalling. A few of them were already holding their noses. Frau Schwanneke seemed to have lost her sense of smell. She was still grinning in all directions.

The next year she had Claudia in her class. Nowadays

that wasn't even allowed. Although lots of colleagues had had their own children in class. Claudia certainly hadn't suffered as a result. You knew where you belonged. You had your income. You knew your child was being looked after.

'But this . . . this is not a void. These are unopened rooms of possibility . . .' He was already talking like Thiele. The same gestures, the same drama. The moon and the stars.

'So much room – room for innovation, room for ideas!' He spread his hands. He should have been a pastor. Pastor Kattner. The Sunday sermon on a Wednesday.

At last she realised where the stench was coming from. The ginkgo tree! And it hadn't occurred to her before! It was the ripened fruits, the rotting flesh. An acrid, rancid smell. The monster of a tree was a leftover from the old school garden, intended as an ornament. With a plaque and an epigram. Split. Neither deciduous nor evergreen. Grown from a seed in Goethe's anniversary year, 1982. Goethe tree. Goethe bone. He had really thought he had discovered the intermaxillary bone. Investigated the investigable. You could only tell if it was a male or a female plant after twenty years, when it bore its first fruits. Almost like sea urchins. The ginkgo had been sexually mature for a few years, and contaminated the air every autumn. Bloody gymnosperm.

'The future of this region, dear pupils, depends on you.'

Appeals to the consciousness. Young people, hear the signals! Failure as a stroke of luck.

'Your generation is the one that . . .'

Everything always depended on the coming generations. Youth was being sold the future all over again.

The wind was unfavourable. The stench was unbearable. You could hammer copper nails into the trunk. But it probably wouldn't die even then. You couldn't finish those trees off. Living fossils like the motionless giant lizards on the Galapagos Islands. A ginkgo had even survived Hiroshima. They could live to a thousand. Like those enormous trees that they'd wanted to visit with Claudia in America. But then they didn't head north. Prehistoric trees. The country was one big primordial landscape. Everything too big, too far. Valleys and deserts, day-long trips, week-long trips. Far too confusing. They'd had every opportunity when they discovered and settled that continent. And what had it produced in the end? Houses made of wood and cardboard. On the other hand, even Claudia's house was massive. Wardrobes as big as rooms, five-lane motorways, neglected pavements and roads with the same names as television series. And towns that could exist only because air conditioning had been invented. The tour guide with one of those ingenuous American faces in which you could still discern the remnants of the faces of European emigrants. A people of immigrants. Claudia translated. She was for ever telling you to look around. She talked about the water all the time. The water that had once been here, the mighty ocean. And claimed that this desert had been nothing but the bottom of a huge sea, and those bizarre, red mountains had been an undersea range. But the only thing there was a dead landscape. Cacti, with holes drilled by the woodpeckers that nested in them. Later, in the reservation, fat Indian women sat outside residential trailers. A fence around infertile land, on which they appeared to be stacking plastic bags. You couldn't look at them, you couldn't take pictures of their graves. Signs all over the place telling you not to do things. Land of the free.

The bell rang. End of morning break. But not long enough for Kattner. Last time he had overrun by several minutes as well. The power of the dictator. Preaching democracy and enforcing his own will. It didn't matter what you called it. It was anything but fair.

'Go wild! Stay here! Change something!' She knew that. Towards the end all speeches broke down into slogans. No form of government was supreme. It would all sort itself out in the end.

Aunt Anita had meant well with her. A huge portion. Königsberg meatballs. Tried and tested school dinners. The plate was full to the brim. You had to be careful that the sauce didn't drip on the lino.

She was early. The teachers' table was still empty. A few pupils at the back. It was practically peaceful. Alone at last. It was even quite tasty.

A bunch of keys rattled on to the table. With a plaited ribbon attached.

'Bon appétit, everybody!' Enter Schwanneke. 'I'll be back in a tick. I've just got to . . .'

Why did she even ask? A haunting. You weren't safe

from her anywhere. She still seemed to be in a bubbling good mood. Inspired by Kattner's sermon. She sat down and peeled herself out of her coat.

'The headmaster's right. We really never learn, do we?'

What a parrot. Always had to repeat everything.

'We really go to school for our whole lives.' She unfolded her napkin and draped it in her lap.

The food slowly went cold. She didn't seem to be very hungry. Perhaps she was on a diet. Women like that were always on a diet. I haven't cooked anything, but look at me lying there.

'Frau Schwanne-k-e?' The way the pupils always had of stretching the last syllable out for ever. Luckily it didn't work with Inge's name.

A girl. Small nose, big eyes. Thin lips. Judging by her politeness, Year Ten. They only used the familiar *du* after Year Eleven.

'Ye-e-es?' The same exaggerated emphasis. Frau Schwanneke turned the whole of her torso. Extra slowly. How she enjoyed it.

'Do we really have to perform the poem tomorrow?'

'But Karoline, that's what we agreed.'

'I've only got the beginning of it.'

'Well that's great. Then tomorrow in class we'll discuss where to take it from there. All right?'

First-class favour-currying.

'Thank you, Frau Schwanneke.'

An inch away from a curtsey. She couldn't really be as sweet as that.

'Ah yes, those dear pupils . . .' Pensive singsong. She crushed her potatoes.

'They're all my children in one way or another.'

You didn't even need to listen. It was always the same song. The fork wandered to the lips. At last she stuffed a mouthful in.

'Some of them you just have to . . .' she chewed as she talked '. . . I've realised this recently – you have to love them . . .' she swallowed. '. . . in order to bear them.' She should be careful. Bits of food could easily get caught in the windpipe of a talking animal.

'When they're standing in front of you, so tiny and despondent, sometimes even a little bit cheeky, then there are actually only two real possibilities . . .'

She was living proof that man differed from the animals not through reason, but through the demonstrative ability to speak.

'Clear off or . . .'

That look. As if she was apologising.

'. . . love.'

This person knew no shame. Her lipstick had worn away already, but the outlines were still there. Pale powder stuffing the pores. The longing for a big stage.

'. . . and I've always opted for love.'

Pathos in the voice. She should really have been an actress. And she was one. Getting publicly drunk on her own hormonal variations.

'I think exchanging thoughts is really something very beautiful. And . . .' Coquettish laugh. Those teeth. Terrifying.

'. . . something very intimate.'

Why was she telling her this? What did she want? No spotlights far and wide, no prospect of applause. But a person without a sense of smell lacked any other intuition.

'Pedagogical Eros.' Schwanneke smacked her lips lasciviously.

Of course, anyone who told the children to call her by her first name also took them to bed for a cuddle. Firm sports-teacher grip. Leaping to assistance when the sport shorts were too short. Pulling down children's knickers. School for touching. They always wanted to do that.

'Ah.' Hand to mouth. Schwanneke was suddenly horrified.

'I'd clean forgotten that I've stopped eating meat.' She rolled a meatball to the edge of the plate. Impossible to look away.

Claudia had also had a phase like that. Wolfgang had just lost his job. Animal production was winding down. And his daughter stopped eating meat. Tasteless. But Inge Lohmark didn't do anyone special favours. Either at school or at home. Claudia didn't stick it out for long. The meatball rolled back.

'I mean, it's just a drain on the environment. The greenhouse effect. Those are the real climate killers. All that methanol.'

So dumb it hurt. Where had she picked that up? She probably hadn't been able to sleep at night, and had been droned to unconsciousness by a particularly meaningful television voice. Used to be the hole in the ozone layer.

Hadn't heard anything about that for ages. Now it was climate change. Over the few billion years of the earth's history there had been climate changes before. Without warming, human beings wouldn't even exist. But this unbearable inflection in the ecological chapter. So guilty. Just designed to propagate a bad conscience. Apocalypse the day after tomorrow. Like in church. Except without heaven. Morality had exactly as little business in biology as it did in politics. As if humans were the only creatures that destroyed their environment. All organisms did. Every species used up space and resources and left waste behind. Every creature deprived another of living space. Where one body was, no other could be. Birds built nests, bees honeycombs, humans prefabs. There was no natural equilibrium. The cycle of matter that kept everything alive was produced only by equilibrium. The sun that rose every day. A massive dip in energy that kept us alive. Equilibrium, that was the end, death.

But now Schwanneke was starting to divide the meatball with her fork.

'Poor animals.' She groaned. As if she meant the meatball.

How stupid could a person actually be? And survival in the wilderness wasn't a walk in the park either; death was brutal out there. A violent death was the most natural thing in the world. And what, excuse me, were we supposed to do with all the animals, the results of selective and controlled breeding? Cattle were a human invention. They were milk machines, grazing flesh with seven stomachs. We had bred them. Now we had to eat them too.

'They have it good. When's your daughter actually coming home?'

'Soon.'

Snake in the grass.

How apparently casually she placed her question. Knife in the back. What did she imagine? 'And your husband?' There we have it. Bull's eye. The potato fell from the fork back on to the plate. Clatter of cutlery. With any luck that would be that.

'He has someone else.' Of course. Compulsion to confess.

'She's younger.'

Trousers down.

'And she's pregnant now, too.'

Not exactly original.

'I can't have one.'

If you knew no shame, you couldn't have children. Self-exposure drained the brain.

'When I was little, I asked my mother how you get pregnant.' She breathed in deeply. She'd be forcing people to talk on her deathbed. What else?

'And then my mother said . . .' Her mouth quivered. She couldn't shut up now. The way the very people who boasted of their tact had to force their emotions on you so obtrusively. '. . . if you really want it to happen.' There was no stopping her now. Really uninhibited. And she was already stripped naked. Don't look. It only encourages them.

'Inge.' She hunched her shoulders.

'Inge.' Lip movements. Barely a voice. She wasn't crying or anything, was she?

'May I call you Inge?'

This was blackmail. All deliberate.

'Yes, you may.' What were you supposed to say? The hydrological cycle was powerful. Lunchtime abuse.

What was going on? A sob. Her thin hands. Schwanneke threw her arms around her. An embrace. A vice-like grip. Her breasts, soft and warm.

The pupils who lived outside town had congregated at the bus stop quite early. The baker on the corner had already shut up shop. The only place near school where you could still get rid of your pocket money was the cigarette machine on Steinstrasse.

The boys tapped listlessly around on their mobile phones, the girls hopped from foot to foot to the music on their headphones, unobtrusively. Even Ellen was being left in peace, immersed in a book. Not a car to be seen. A Sunday atmosphere in the middle of the week. What was missing was Erika.

So where was she? Inge Lohmark positioned herself in such a way that she had a view both of the city side and the way to school. The embankment, the road to the market. Nothing. The bus came. Everybody got on board. Not even a scramble. The bus driver's stupid face. She looked round again.

'Drive on. I've forgotten something.'

The doors closed.

The bus drove off. Without her.

Jennifer's baffled face through the glass. What now? It was really cold. And so dark. November weather. Cross the road.

The school corridor was in darkness. All lessons over. And no evening classes yet. Slender iron bars, a grille, upstairs. A hand on the banister. The cast-concrete stones of the windowsills.

She had gone alone back then. She hadn't talked to anybody about it. Who could she have talked to? The thing with Hanfried was over. And it had nothing to do with Wolfgang. A purely pelvic business. A minor operation and an overnight stay in hospital. His head was full anyway. It had been an uneasy time. The borders open. The money new. For decades plant production had been granted preference. The tables had turned now. Revolt of the livestock-breeders. No one knew where it went from there. Just people claiming they had no idea. First of all, what it meant was that a new dairy facility was being built. And that they were to switch to supplementary feeding. The doctor thought she was past it. But then he'd done it anyway. The interim arrangement applied. He was handsome, although he had a bald patch. Certainly not from here. His few hairs stood up like short electric wires. The nurse shaved her pubic hair and held her hand. Until the injection took effect. The first thing she saw when she woke up was the frosted glass of the hospital windows. The ribbed panes in the door. Like the kitchen door at her parents' house. A veil of spiders' webs. Thin parchment pages in photograph albums. A frog goes into a dairy shop. The saleswoman asks, Well, little frog, what would you like?

The frog says, Quark. Made Claudia laugh every time. Even as a child. And even later, too. Her favourite joke. Was there such a thing as a dairy shop? In the old days, perhaps. The dairies had closed down overnight. They didn't know what to do with the milk. At school everyone drank coke. And when they wanted to hand over the cattle after the grazing period, the way they did every year, there was no abattoir. And no stalls for the winter. They had no idea what to do with the cattle. Fly-by-night traders bought them for a pittance. They poured the milk on the fields. She couldn't have managed another child. Claudia was going through puberty. And Wolfgang was fighting for his job. To give milk, a cow had to have calved. Only a cow that gave milk was a cow. And only a woman who had given birth to a child was a woman. Antibodies. False rhesus factor. It just hadn't worked. She had given birth to Claudia and fed her. She had fulfilled her duty. What else could she have done? Breastfeeding was out. She hadn't had any milk. Her pubic hair quickly grew back. Amazing that it was happy only to grow to a certain length in some parts of your body. The genetic programme.

How cold she felt all of a sudden, a shiver down her back, gooseflesh on her head. But that was normal. A relic from prehistoric times, when humans still had fur. The erect hairs made you look stronger if you were facing an enemy. There was no enemy. Everything was fine. What was normality anyway? Sometimes the exception was the rule. Flowerless plants, parthenogenesis in aphids. Flightless birds. She could get divorced. Never occurred to her.

Rattling noises. A door was open. A cleaning woman was

stacking the chairs. That they still had to wear those Dederon aprons. Floor polish. Smelled even worse than the ginkgolic acid.

She hadn't really noticed Hanfried at first. A local initiative. At last a *Subbotnik* who was really doing voluntary work. Wolfgang didn't join in. He found it too tricky. They cleared the rubbish out of the kettle-holes and planted trees along the forest path behind the new block. Arable hard shoulders. Hans had been there at first. Claudia too. Along with the vicar's rail-thin children.

Hanfried always fetched the trees. Grafting stock. Field maples, beeches, chestnuts. From the forester. Sometimes she came along. She really hadn't expected to fall pregnant again. Forgotten that she could still have children. Claudia was already having her period. The cycle of the ripening egg. It had nothing to do with her any more. In fact it only occurred to her later. When she had to sign for the X-ray: not pregnant. An interruption, as if you could resume the pregnancy at some point later on. Have this child some other time. She had lost both children. The unborn and the born. Nonsense. You couldn't even think that. The trees had been ploughed over long ago.

Perhaps because she had kissed the hand of that statue. Costa Brava. Her first real trip abroad. To a monastery in the mountains. The worship of the black Madonna. Health and fertility. Not that she believed in anything like that. Maternal love was a hormone. A myth. The stout goddess from a hungry time, older than arable farming. The Venus of Willendorf. Squat limestone body, huge drooping breasts above a fat maternal belly, enormous backside. Little curls instead of a face. Fertility in its purest state.

The door to the headmaster's study was open. His secretary only worked half-days. Now Kattner was sitting in her place.

'Frau Lohmark? What are you doing here?'

'I forgot something.' Again. As if she had something to hide.

'What?'

Just use his own tactics. Answer his question with another one. 'And you?'

'Crossword puzzle.' He held up his newspaper.

'Egyptian god of the Realm of the Dead.'

Was that a question?

'Austrian actress, thirteen letters.'

No idea.

'All right then. What have we here? Hang on a second. First man, starts with A.'

'Ape.' It came out automatically. Like a reflex.

Kattner snorted. 'Ape! Don't believe it.' He rolled his chair away from the table and threw back his head.

Now the right answer occurred to her.

'Ape. Ape. Ape.' He wouldn't calm down.

'Frau Lohmark, for that you get a gold star.' He spread out his arms. 'Sit down here.'

The chair was uncomfortable.

Kattner rolled back to the desk.

'And by the way, there's something I wanted to say to you.'

Always these artificial pauses.

'So, chemistry will soon be moving into your classroom, not that you'll be surprised.'

'And why's that?'

'Well, the arts course really needs a room with a basin. Must have something to do with paint. And Frau Schwanneke's not going to give up hers. You can imagine. As a rule: biology and chemistry go hand in glove.'

Chemistry was mute. Biology spoke. She hadn't been particularly good at chemistry. Citric-acid cycle. Electron transport chain. She might miss chemistry. But not in her room. The stench in the playground was bad enough.

'No one has so far seen an atom through a microscope.' That was what her seminar leader had always said.

'No, they have. Didn't you know?' He seemed quite horrified. 'They can make molecules visible with electron microscopes.'

Oh, yes, that's right. She'd read that somewhere.

'Doesn't matter. I wasn't particularly good at chemistry either. Could never tell if it was a model or reality.' A chummy grin. 'I always got a three. What's that thing they say? Three is satisfactory. And what could be nicer than being satisfied?' He was almost singing it. 'Isn't that right?'

'I haven't had any further training for ages.' The last she'd had must have been ten years ago.

'Inge, I get it. It's not really worth it any more.'

'So who's been going round saying that you should go to school all your life?'

'So you should. And the last thing I want is to doubt your specialist competence. But 90 per cent of teachers in this nation of ours are over forty. You can't imagine what that means.'

'A lot of experience.'

'Totally antiquated. Of course old people are the future. Not least economically. The only growing market. And biologically speaking the sixty-year-olds are younger than forty-year-olds twenty years ago.'

A little flag in the wind.

'But you know: the battle for existence. You're an expert in this one. A bit of fresh air would do us all good. Survival of the fittest!' He rubbed his hand across his stomach.

'As you know, there's a lot of uncertainty about what's going to happen to us all, well, not me . . . over the next four years. It might even be advisable to start looking around for an alternative sphere of activity.'

What was he getting at?

'Neubrandenburg, for example.'

What was he talking about?

'Of course if that happened you would keep your specialist area.'

Specialist area? What was he talking about?

'Or . . .' he took a deep breath. '. . . or you would stay here in the town.'

'The middle school?' Wild horses. That was blackmail.

'No, no. They're oversubscribed anyway. A much better idea: back to your roots. By which I mean: you could start right over from the beginning.'

None of it made any sense.

'Primary school!'

He seemed to have gone mad. It would sort itself out in a minute. She had nothing to fear. The intelligent animal waits.

'And excuse me, what would I teach at primary school?' This was completely out of order. Sorting out people's personal affairs.

'Well, general studies. You're exactly right for that. Forest, house, people. Measuring temperatures. Studying clouds. Looking for mushrooms. You could finally provide the essentials that you miss at the moment. I mean, that's why you became a teacher. To teach the children something.'

That certainly wasn't why she'd become a teacher.

'You know: they pay unemployment benefit for two years. And there are enough similar tasks that are less gratifying: looking after people with learning difficulties. Night watch in the nuthouse. Shift work in the children's home.'

He couldn't do a thing to her. The socialist personality is formed primarily by the labour process. Working to rule. Chinese labourers jumping from high-rises because they'd been fired. A father killing his whole family because he had lost his job. Debts that could never be paid. Did they still even have children's homes? Man was the great working animal. No life without work. Why had she become a teacher?

'But of course that's all just pie in the sky. For the time being, of course, you're here. It was just a thought.'

But upsetting the apple-cart. Because her parents had

said it would suit her. Because you have to quote a profession to get into extended secondary school. Because children were born and teachers needed. Always. At least in the old days.

'But what's really up with you? Your car must have been back out of the garage for ages. Why are you still taking the bus?'

'Ecology.'

A frown. He didn't believe a word of it.

'You look dreadful, Lohmark. I worry about you. You seem exhausted. You look tired. Relax. Do a course in something. In the old Russian room there's make-up at half-past three, I think. Wait, I'll just check.' He fished a bit of crushed yellow paper from one of the piles.

She had to go straight away. There was no point sitting here a moment longer and being humiliated by this circus ringmaster. The next bus didn't leave till six. From tomorrow she would start taking the car again. Why was she still sitting here?

Kattner gave her a challenging look.

Her body, weak. Her head, so heavy. Her brain was devouring all her energy. The sea squirt, a spineless tunicate, simply amputated its head as soon as it grew up and became sedentary. Jellyfish had no brains either. They got through life perfectly well with only a nerve system. That head. Too big even for childbirth. A storehouse of knowledge, as oversized as the antlers of the ice-age giant deer, the mammoth's tusks, the long canines of the sabre-tooth tiger. A millstone. A cul-de-sac. Eventually. What was the point of it? That accumulation of knowledge. What we didn't know, and what we didn't know yet, and everything we would know in future. Undisciplined weeds. Further education didn't help you much with that. You couldn't work it out in the end. It all just got more complex and complicated. So much was still unexplored. There were still open questions in biology. The intricate relationships between the species, not yet understood. Some hypotheses were true together, even though future experiments would reveal them to be false. That they'd believed the mystery of life was a novel. Just because its alphabet consisted of four letters. What were novels anyway? Illustrations of philosophies. The blueprints had been decoded, but nothing was understood. A secret script. Just units that produced a word from time to time, pearls on a chromosomal chain. Pearls before swine. If the organism really was just a slave of its genes, then its master was beyond understanding. All the things lying about. In the DNA. And in the RNA. Transcripts of unknown functions, temporarily inoperative pseudogenes. Appendices and interstices. Intelligence wasn't equally divided even among monozygotic twins. From the genetic point of view, we didn't even remain identical to ourselves throughout our lifetimes. The schoolbooks needed to be rewritten, they needed to be expanded, because more knowledge was constantly being produced. New studies. No knowledge. Reason didn't make us any more intelligent. Forced into a causal straitjacket, the self as a neuronal illusion, a really elaborate multimedia show. You would need to be an animal. A real animal. Without a consciousness to inhibit the will. Animals always knew what they were doing. Or rather, they didn't need to know. If in danger, the lizard shed its tail. Just dumping unwanted ballast. That you always had to think about what you needed to do next, how best to behave. Animals knew their needs, they had an instinct. Hungry or full, tired or awake, anxious or ready to mate. They just did it. They followed the herd, they swam to the source, lay yawning in the sun or in the shade, as the case may be. Ate themselves a layer of fat. Hibernated.

Kattner clicked the desk lamp on. It was dark now. The light fell on his mouth. Eyes in the shade. Where had her instinct gone? How had she got here? Where was the tail that she could shed right now?

Evolution Theory

The sun emerged from behind the trees, and now hung over the forest. Everything stood out, clear and undimmed; blossoming pussy-willows and white-tipped sloes, bright yellow forsythias and thin green-branched birches. It had done nothing but rain for days. But this morning the sky was deep blue and almost cloudless. It was reflected in the puddles of the watermeadows. They were huge, big as lakes. It would soon be Easter. Ten days. High time too. How calm it was, quite peaceful. Barely a car. No schoolchildren at the side of the road. The bus had stopped ages ago. The bus stops deserted. As if they had fallen out of use years before.

The window stuck as she tried to wind it down. Sooner or later she was going to need a new car. But Wolfgang had just bought himself an incubator. It held forty eggs. The breeding season had already started. It was cool, but the sun still burned on the skin. It would be warm today. Soft west wind. Spring. Almost summery. Even the lime trees already had bright tips. The forest floor was scattered white with wood anemones. The barley abundantly green, almost blue. A dark silhouette against the light. Someone was stomping across the field, hands clasped behind his back. Bent forward, taking small steps, as if he were fighting against the air resistance. She took her foot off the accelerator. Beside this figure, a scurrying patch, a small, reddish-brown animal. Tail held vertical, bent at the end, counterbalancing the skipping movements. It could only be a cat. Hans. Now she recognised him. It was Hans. With Elisabeth, running through the grass, making little jumps from time to time so as not to fall behind him. A couple that had found each other.

He had got it right. You just hauled your way along from holiday to holiday. Ten days without that weary pack. Ten days that she would have all to herself. Just the garden. The house. And Hans, of course. Their daily conversations by the garden fence. In fact only he had found his place. At home, in his cave, with the two outside thermometers and the weather report keeping him in check. A pensioner's existence. Terrible, in fact. She had to get away. To the Ivenack Oaks. They were at least as old as Claudia's Californian giants. If not even older. To the chalk cliffs or the flint fields. Strolls on the beach. It wasn't that far. The free-run enclosure with the fallow deer. Their white dappled fur.

What was the bus doing over there? In the middle of the road. Blue and white stripes, with black tinted windows. It actually was the school bus. It had clearly stopped. The children were standing around it. Bright anoraks in the roadside ditch. In the field, Kevin and consorts. Looked quite contented. Of course. At last something had happened. A few girls were even playing Chinese skipping in the street. Noise and scuffling. In the middle of it, Marie Schlichter's bus-stop face. The driver walked around the bus, a mobile phone to his ear. Ellen by his side. Now he opened a flap and stuck his head inside. And there was Jennifer. She came closer and waved at her, she wanted to say something. At last the opposite carriageway was clear. Speed up and overtake.

The day was over. Half of it would come too late. But she would still deal with the subject matter; evolution until before Whitsun. Then summary and outlook. A shame that there was no centralised teaching plan any more. Today each Bundesland had its own books and its own Abitur. A misunderstanding of flexibility. As if different natural laws applied in Bavaria. The nerve system remained central. That wasn't freedom. Everyone did his own thing. Before, you were at most two weeks behind the teaching material. You could always catch up. Now, if you moved house, you were lost. But you were lost anyway. Lucky she was driving a car again. In the old days she'd even hitch-hiked into the Riesengebirge. No one did that any more. That was all she needed. On a big trip with the pack. An involuntary hiking day. And she'd once even wished for it to happen. An accident. Emergency. Stable lateral position. Life and death. But no one was injured. No ambulance, no wailing siren. Nothing happened. And if it did, then it wasn't really serious. Scraped knees. By the wedding everything was fine again. You didn't die as quickly as that. Father's words. My eye. He himself had just keeled over. He'd been spared it all. The *Wende*, the fall of the Wall. Turning away from the light. By the time the ambulance came at last, it was all over. Mother, on the other hand. Years of. She died his death all over again. Illness retroactively, a double dose. All that chattering. When I'm no longer here. That was blackmail. A trick to provoke a contradiction. The way they all got so soft in old age. Side-effect a horror of death. Suddenly regretting what had never been called into question in all those years. Giving in on the last few yards, caving in. Just because the bodily functions gradually ceased to perform their functions. The slack hands. Skin like parchment.

There was the next bus stop. Saskia with a few guys from the middle school. Headphones on. Hands in their trouser pockets. All dressed up and nowhere to go. Could be a while. The black wooden hut behind them like a giant dog kennel. Animals on a leash. That was exactly what they were. As far as the chain stretched. The radius was staked out. In space, in time. Day after day. The sandy ground, stamped firm from all that waiting. A few holes dug. Buried bones.

There was the turn-off. The yellow arrow pointing into the forest. Indicator on. Brake. She turned into it. The road in shadows. Cold air. Window up again. Spruce trees. Yellow needles on the forest floor. Branches against a black background. Hand in front of her eyes. No oncoming traffic. Fleeing. Bull by the horns. A few houses. Cracked tarmac. Rainwater still in the potholes. Another farmyard. For sale. Cobblestones. The last village. Low fences, closed curtains. Deserted. There she was. She was really standing there. Of course. Where else? Face against the window.

Door open.

'Get in. The bus has broken down.'

She sat down, forced her rucksack between her knees, pulled the door shut, reached for the seatbelt and fastened herself in. The engine wailed. Too much acceleration. She didn't even look. Not a word. The stork bite. On her collar the outward-turned lining of her blue windcheater. Red-dish patches on her bare neck. The pale shimmer of her scalp under her brown hair. Only the hum of the engine.

All the rubbish in the glove compartment, in the tray between the seats. As if there was something there that might give her away. As if she had whoknowswhat plans for her. Only a visiting card from Wolfgang, her fat bunch of keys, a few cough sweets. Sea-buckthorn flavour. Corruption of a minor. Turn on the radio? No, rather not. Just a distraction. Fresh air. Open the window another crack. Air to breathe. That was better. Outside, scattered trees in the fields.

'They're holes from the ice age.'

No. At last she turned round. She belonged to her.

'The clumps of trees in the fields and those boggy sink-holes date from the ice age. They were left over when the glaciers retreated. And when the blocks of ice thawed, they formed these holes in the earth, sometimes even caves under the earth. The agricultural cooperatives used to fill them up so that it was easier for the tractors to drive evenly across the fields. But they kept filling up with water again. They're so deep, they reach all the way back to the ice age. You simply can't dry them up. Very important biotopes, by the way.'

Erika pretended to scratch her shin, oblivious as a child, shameless. Was there such a thing as female paedophilia?

'Have you ever seen a fawn? I mean, in the wild?'

'Nope, why?'

'As a child I once found a fawn in a clump of trees like that. In the bushes under an elevated hide. We looked right at one another, the fawn and I. It was absolutely beautiful, and right there, perhaps only a couple of feet away. I would only have needed to stretch my hand out to stroke it. Its fur was reddish-brown with white dots. But of course I didn't touch it. I'm sure you know this: its mother would have rejected it. Because of the strange smell.'

She shifted about on the seat. Knees pressed together. Who knows? Perhaps she was scared. After all, she could do anything she liked with her. Anything – what was that supposed to mean? What did she want from her? The ostrich silhouette on Wolfgang's visiting card. The keys, the sweets. Nothing had happened to her yet. Nobody had seen her. And what would she want to do with her? Into the forest, into the hides, into the kettle-holes. Hand in hand. Whether she wanted to or not. Lock her in. Leave her out. Somewhere. Just like that. Child abduction. Was she even a child? A minor, anyway. Not especially pretty. She was in her hands now. Who had trapped whom? Why had she picked up a schoolgirl? What happened next? She could hardly throw her out here. She had probably made a mistake. Misrepresentation of the facts. Cooperation unsatisfactory. She wasn't interested in anything. She was no better than the rest. She just stared straight ahead. Dull. Went along with everything. As she was supposed to! Tie her to a tree. Force her to watch. To give an answer at last. Perhaps a fawn might come by. That's what she would get. Stuff her mouth full so that she never said anything ever again. The way she just sat there like that. Breathing. As if nothing had happened. And nothing had happened. There was nothing more to say.

Outside the gleaming white wind turbines, circling tirelessly. On a boggy field, even a few lost swans. Brightly coloured rubbish in the box trees, plastic bags in the bushes. In the garden colony the wild tulips blazed already. Outside the car showroom fluttering flags. The tender shadows of the branches on the façades. Her spot in the teachers' car park was free as ever. She pulled on the handbrake. Erika loosened her belt, picked up her rucksack, got out, slammed the door shut. Far too loudly.

'Morning!' To top it all. Frau Schwanneke, sailing along on her red bicycle.

'Hello, Inge.' She grinned. Knowingly. She had seen everything. In a car. A little flaw. Enough. Once and for all.

'Good morning.' A skeleton crew today, then. And no sign of the rest of the gang. Literally fallen by the wayside. This wasn't a lesson any more, it was coaching. Not even a squadron of flu viruses had managed that in all those years. A few dogged characters, dazzled by the morning sun. But as long as the reflexes worked. It took two to have a biology lesson as well.

'Sit down.'

Work to rule. Just don't make any exceptions any more. In the theatre, too, they performed as long as the audience was in the majority. And they still were, in the majority: six against one. Erika and the five chaps from town. And on stage, just her: Frau Lohmark. So: curtain up.

'Open your books, page one hundred and seventy-one.'

On a single page in front of them was everything that lay behind them: the march of life through the earth's ages, depicted as the spiral whorls of a snail's house, from the Archaic to the Quarternary, from nothing to the present, in its various different stages of development and manifestations: sponges, algae, trilobites, brachiopods, invertebrates, echinoderms, muscles, bryozoans, cephalopods, arthropods, armoured fish, dicotyledons, tree-high ferns, marine iguanas, giant dragonflies, coal forests, flying dragons, long-necked giant lizards, primitive horses, sabre-tooth tigers, mammoths and prehistoric man.

At the centre of the spiral was a blackish-grey maw, a vortex into the unimaginably distant past, a maelstrom into the depths of an ocean from which everything grew, dark and misty as all theories of the beginning: Haeckel's primordial slime, Oparin's seething primordial soup, Miller's primordial atmosphere in gas-filled flasks. Where did life come from? A mass of worms from rotten mud. A violent bang. Electrical discharges, organic molecules, billions of protozoa, the building-blocks of life, the leap into time, into space, the beginning of all being: and in the middle a number.

'Three point seven billion years.'

Outrageous. Three point seven billion. Whether she said it or not, it didn't matter at all. It exceeded all imagination. With the best will in the world.

On the teaching schedule it said: convey a sense of time. As if people who feverishly awaited each individual birthday were interested in the age of the earth. They were still too inexperienced to grasp how vanishingly small their time on earth was, how vain their existence, how ridiculously insignificant every moment. They knew nothing.

When you said prehistory, they saw only hissing dinosaurs and shaggy elephants with flashing tusks, giant lizards the size of a house in deadly combat, a Gordian knot of land reptiles with their teeth sunk into the back of their adversaries. Aggressive cavemen in a wintry landscape, on a mammoth hunt. Whittling Neanderthals in furs by the campfire. They would never learn to think in millions of years. Never understand that all the life surrounding them was the product of tiny steps over monstrously long periods of time. An immeasurable, chronic, tedious process of transformation that could not be observed, not experienced, just deduced from clues assembled with enormous difficulty. And no numbers helped either, no dizzyingly long column of numbers. This was the final destination. The brain cut out. And your imagination does you no good either. Certainly not that.

'Multicellular life developed only about five hundred million years ago. Previously, life was monocellular. For three billion years the earth had been inhabited only by very simple bacteria-like creatures.' Until today, the most successful form of existence, a freeloading life, a lasting form, the true rulers of the world. In all that time bacteria and viruses hadn't had to develop any further. They were immortal and perfect. No brain, no nerves. Only something perfect didn't need to develop any further. Development was only an expression of imperfection. The directed, irreversible change from the fertilised egg-cell via several stages to death. The very fact that man had to go to school said volumes about the inadequacy of his construction. Almost all other animals were ready at birth. Ready for life. A match for it. After a few hours they were already standing on their own feet. Human beings, on the other hand, remained unfinished all their lives. Deficient creatures. Runts. Physiological premature births that have reached sexual maturity. Unprepared by nature. Only ready for life right at the end. You only grew so old because you had such an infinite amount to learn.

'Your homework was to assign animals and plants to the individual eras. So, Ferdinand: what were things like in the Ordovician?'

He cleared his throat. The voice-breaking gods had finally answered his prayers. 'First vertebrates, jawless . . .'

'Whole sentences, please.'

'Erm . . . For the first time vertebrates, jawless fish, shell-fish, corals and sea urchins. And algae . . .'

'Those still aren't whole sentences.'

'. . . algae are developing.'

'You forgot jellyfish. They're developing too. You mustn't forget them. The Ordovician sea was full of shimmering jellyfish, as was the Cambrian. Like the ones in the corridor.'

'Mhm.' He nodded like a docile pony.

'And how should we imagine the Carboniferous, Annika?' Before she could get even more agitated. Miss Clever-Clogs.

'It saw the emergence of the extensive coal jungles with ferns, forty-metre-high club-moss trees and ten-metre-high horsetails and giant dragonflies. And the primitive reptiles are developing. These include the amphibian fish, the ich-thyostega. It was the first vertebrate to come on land. It was . . .'

'Thank you, thank you, that's enough.'

She really was a pain. People who thought they always had to do the right thing were the most unbearable of all.

'And in the Cretaceous?'

A glance into the class. There was hardly anybody left.

'Jakob.'

Today in his sleeveless vest, his own decal on the front.

'Evergreens . . .' A knock in the corridor. The door flew open, and the horde from the road fell into the classroom. Open jackets, bags in their hands. With bright-red faces and wind-blown hair, as if they'd just climbed a mountain.

'Sit in your places and be as quiet as possible. You have breaktime to get changed. So, Jakob!'

He coughed slightly. Staring at his notes. 'The emergence of evergreen deciduous forests, development of birds, heyday of the dinosaurs.'

'And what happens to them in the end?'

'They die out.' His voice was matter-of-fact, but full of sympathy. Like an undertaker.

'Correct.' More than 99 per cent of all species that ever existed on earth had died out.

But everybody thought only about those ridiculously big forty-tonners with tennis-ball-sized brains, which weren't even capable of regulating their body temperature.

'Yes, that was a real mass-extinction! Three-quarters of

all species of animals and plants disappeared. But you know: the death of one means the birth of the other. And living creatures dying out is one of the most important characteristics of the phylogenic process.' The history of life was basically a history of dying. And every war, every disaster was the start of something new.

It was a cycle. Outside the window, the crowned heads of the chestnut trees. Buds, just before they opened. On some branches, tiny, glistening leaves had peeled out, and now hung slackly, exhausted by the exertions of their birth.

'It was only with the decline of the saurians that the fur-bearing animals became the dominant group of vertebrates. The victory procession of the mammals was beginning. All of a sudden it was advantageous to have fur and warm blood, bring your offspring alive into the world and suckle them on milk. In the fat maternal belly the young are better protected than in an eggshell, however hard it might be. Nest robbery is impossible, but the mother herself is of course in as much danger as any other class of animal.' Maternal mortality. The fatal risks of giving birth. Death in childbirth. Any pregnancy. Profound changes that weakened the body. Shared blood circulation. Too many intoxicants endangered the foetus. Birth was one great injury. The loss of blood alone. Egg-laying was child's play in comparison. Aunt Martha died. Having her fifth child. But in those days every third child died in babyhood. Early selection.

'For every living creature that has withstood the struggle for survival, there are countless competing organisms that have not made it through. We are only here because many others were left by the wayside.' A few weeks before, a man on the city bus had had a heart attack. He was driven around all over the place, back to the terminus over and over again, and back to the little bus station in town. Only in the evening, when the bus went to the depot, did the driver check him. By that time there was nothing more to be done. Being driven around half-dead for twelve hours. If everyone looked after himself, everyone would be looked after.

'When a living creature dies, decay usually sets in. Mites, woodlice and a series of micro-organisms digest the corpse. Mushrooms assume the main task! They count as neither animals nor plants. They divided off from the rest very early on. They have a realm all to themselves. They are a third life form!' Descendants of a protozoan, just like us. Pioneering settlers of the primordial continent.

'I'm not talking here about chanterelles or the fancy mushrooms that you fry up in a pan, but all those creatures that ensure that all the refuse, everything dead and dying that accumulates every day, is broken down again. There is nothing that cannot be broken down by some species of mushroom.' They had completely specialised in exploiting the remains of others, only feeding on what was left when others died, even though they had neither a digestive system nor sensory organs. Their significance could not be overstated. And at the same time the decomposers embodied the fundamental principle of life most consistently. Living on the death of others. Of course everything did that. It was the principle of all life,

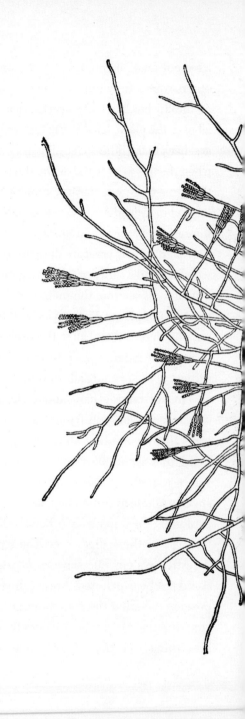

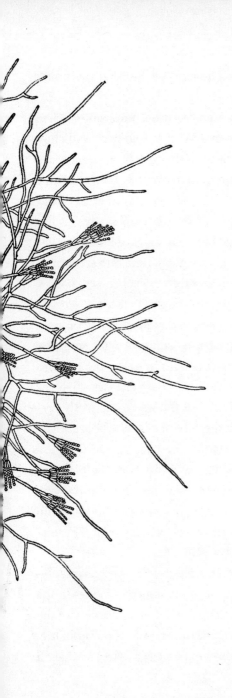

however highly developed it might be. But that was taboo, no one wanted to notice.

'But a few organisms are spared decomposition. Their remains survive the eras in a layer of sediment and show posterity what had once been. If they can be found in excavations.' Unelected representatives of their species. Prehistoric ten-foot crabs in silvery shimmering shale, black conifers in clay, primitive fish with fat scales like glazed ceramics. Flattened between layers of limestone like dried flowers. Pressed by the weight of time into an impression, just a shadow of themselves. Bleached-out bodies. Dried-up corpses. Crushed into images. True art. Children's treasures. The petrified sea urchin that Mother had brought from Yugoslavia, the leg of a mosquito caught in glassy amber. Thousands of thunderstones in cases, the remains of extinct squid. Fruits from the Tertiary era – small, black and round as rabbit pellets – all the way to perfectly preserved mammoths from the Siberian Arctic coast. Deep frozen and stone dead. Hadn't she been to see that film with Claudia, in which a man was frozen in the pack ice, and thawed decades later? And then they had to sort everything out specially for him as it had been in his day: thin moustaches, farthingales and coaches in the park. The television hidden in the antique cabinet.

'It's only because there are fossils that we know about earlier life at all. They are the most important clues to the process of evolution, the theory of the changeability of the species, their common origins, the enormous power of tiny steps – but an unimaginably long time ago! The fact that all life is interrelated and nothing is separate from anything else, that everything belongs together, even if it doesn't look that way.' A theory without numbers, formulae or experiments. Anyone who understood it had understood life, had solved the mystery of the world. That was what Kattner should have delivered his sermon about.

'Fossils are the witnesses of evolution, the transitional animals its crown witnesses.' A process of evidence. But it was a long drawn-out procedure; the taking of evidence would never be complete. Time and again, new, ancient traces would be found, surprising witnesses called, impossible animals: the coelacanth, which had died out in the Cretaceous, and then arisen from the dead. The platypus, an imagined creature, the sum of foreign parts. A suckling monotreme, a loner that had split away from the rest early on, a living link between all kinds of species. A creature from those children's books in which head, chest and bottom can be endlessly reassembled: little button eyes, tiny ear-slits and a duck's bill, webbed feet and a beaver's tail. Nothing fitted together, and yet it was alive. A dead branch amidst flourishing shrubs, or the supporting branch in the family tree, the crucial fork? An insult to the healthy human mind.

Lately, the brightly coloured periodic table had hung proudly on the back wall of the classroom, the formulas packed in colourful little boxes. Nice and clean. Tidied away. Mankind was still a gatherer, the only kind of the genus Homo that survived and had retrospectively to create order that nature had not provided. There were two

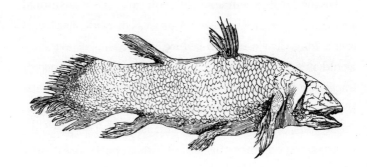

strategies for dealing with life. Simply to take it as it came, or try to understand it. Create a synoptic view. Bring light into darkness. Beat a path through the thicket. So many gaps in the chain of fossil findings had to be traced, so many yawning gulfs bridged between two classes of animals. All that undergrowth. The hope of giving an account of phylogeny once again. Tracing the lost common forefather of two species, the missing links, the ancestor of the whale, a land animal that returned to the sea. But they did know where to look. Everything was known, just undiscovered.

Fossil fragments, reassembled. A few bones in the spotlight. Grinning skulls, getting bigger and bigger. Again a few cubic centimetres' more room for the brain mass, the highest of all innards, dangerously overestimated. Four mammal skeletons in the development of man. The apelike ancestor who rears up and loses his fur. Swaps the ability to climb for standing on two legs. A pair of flat feet. But the hands are free. Work can begin. Bulges above the eyebrows. Wide jaw. The image of monkey shaven from head to toe. It looked like an old man. Our own still-living relations. Chimpanzees in front of the mirror, gorillas in the mist. Perhaps the apes were descended from us? Scientists bent over a handful of bones. Another step in the dark. Ribs with girls' names. The half-skeleton Lucy, the fossil Ida: the lemur-like ur-mammal, a cowering small primate with a damp nose, a wide cat's tail and two crippled vampire hands. In the foetus position. That was how they found it. Rolled up. Needy. Pitiful. The missing link? Hotly desired, painfully missed. Not even a remote great-aunt. Indirectly,

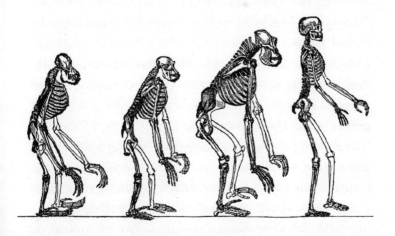

we were related to every clump of cells that had ever existed on earth.

'Please turn the page.' There it was, the primordial bird, the reptile in feathers, the famous transitional animal, the link between two now-separated classes. With bent legs and spread feathers. Two wings, the neck curving backwards. Flattened, as if someone had driven over it. She had seen it. The one in Berlin, the most famous of all fossils. In the museum. Behind glass. A child had asked, Is that an angel?

'The archaeopteryx bears the characteristics of two classes of animal: it has plumage and no beak, but a jaw full of teeth, gripping feet with claws, a misshapen sternum and a spinal column that leads far into the tail. It was no bigger than a pigeon, but could fly no better than a chicken. It clung to tree trunks and plunged down from time to time or fluttered from branch to branch. You couldn't really call it flying.' More pre-bird than primordial. Having feathers didn't mean much. All birds had passed through a winged ancestral stage. From the point of view of evolutionary history, the archaeopteryx was a bird before the ability to fly, and the ostrich a bird after it. Flying reflexes were still present, but they lacked the hard pinions that you need to cut through the air when flying.

'Of course clues to phylogeny may also be found in the human body. They reveal themselves in small, apparently insignificant details. The vermicular appendix. The coccyx. The wisdom teeth.' Atrophied organs, useless characteristics that did little damage and were carried around as

souvenirs from the animal past. The fossils were buried in the body itself. Primitive man lived within us.

'Sometimes there are throwbacks. Then man is overtaken by his past. In some few individuals, characteristics suddenly appear which we discarded long ago. Extra milk glands above and below the breasts, for example. An ear ending in a point, as in cats and dogs. A coccyx that peeps out over the bum like a tail.'

Expressions of disbelief. Probably thought she was making up fairy stories. But that was the truth. We all had to pass through those. Even before birth, even in our mothers' bodies, we had to live through it all, three point seven million years, the whole exhausting evolution of man in nine months. All the ballast stowed in our bones. We were a patchwork, the sum of all previous parts, a stopgap that worked more or less, full of superfluous characteristics. We dragged the past around with us. It made us what we were, and we had to deal with it. Life wasn't a struggle, it was a burden. You had to bear it. As best you could. A task to perform from the first drawn breath. As a human being you were always at work. You never died of an illness, only ever of the past. A past that had not prepared us for this present.

'Anatomically speaking, we're still hunters and gatherers.' Past-time people who loitered around in small groups in the savannah. Human beings were by no means adapted to the present day. They were still stuck in the old stone age. Limping along behind. Only our descendants would be a match for the present. But they would be living in a completely different world, as strange to us as life in a stone-age cave. Outside, the branches rocked in the wind. A tractor drove past, leaving muddy tracks on the tarmac. Just as she'd always thought when she was a child that you could catch up with the others. Just wait two years, then I'll be as old as you.

Desperate trainee teachers who ran out of the classroom and locked themselves in the toilet. Crying jags and breakdowns. Bernburg's burnout. Off sick for weeks. A diagnosis like a triumph. Self-importance. They were all burnt out. It was part of it. Service in the very front line. If you weren't strong enough, you didn't survive in the long term. The big work placement at the end of the fourth year of study. A jump into ice-cold water. The pack could smell your fear. Every week they came up with something new. They had the power. And they were always in the majority. You were alone by yourself at the board. At first wanting to join in with the laughter. Switching sides. Being part of it. But she learned quickly. You had to make a name for yourself. Bull by the horns. Because she would always be standing there by the board, in front of the class, alone. The door was closed. Forty-five minutes could be a very long time. You had to survive it. Concentration. They were constantly lying in wait, determined just to see you fail. Make a mistake and you were lost for ever. Where that was concerned, they had the memory of an elephant. The pack had an excellent network. Your reputation that ran far ahead of you. Just don't make a mistake. Turn the spit. The most important thing was to be strict from the outset. You could still ease up. Theoretically at least. Be hard. Be consistent. No exceptions.

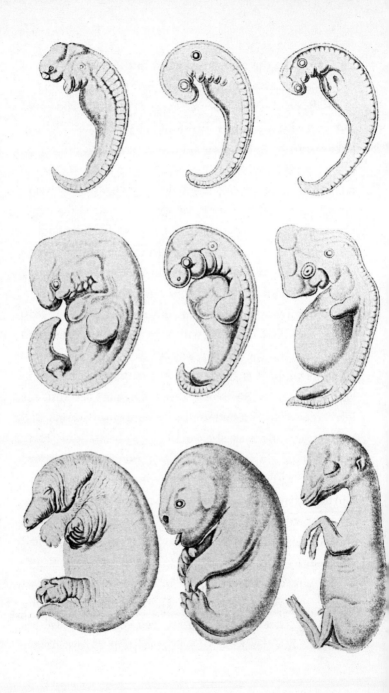

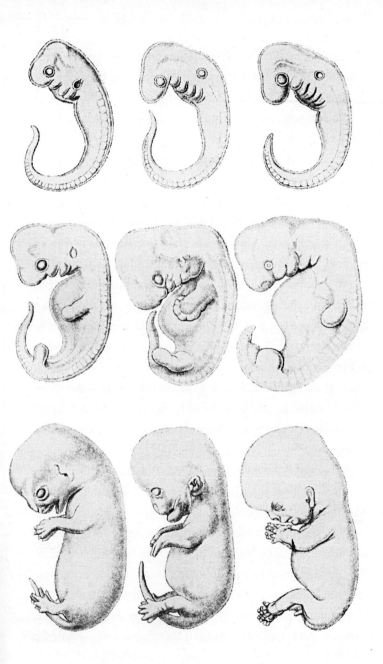

No favourites. Stay unpredictable. Of course pupils were enemies. The lowest in the school fabric. Soon they all knew the name of Lohmark.

'Take hiccups, for example. It's nothing but a leftover from gill breathing.'

Now she'd actually started tapping herself on the sternum.

'The elaborations may be diverse, but the blueprints are very manageable. Flowers have five to six petals, land vertebrates five fingers.' Vertebrates were nothing but worms in reverse. Their intestines were shifted to the front and their nerve systems to the back. Soft on the outside because they had an internal skeleton. Man was a bilateral animal. Two eyes, one heart. Animals with a spinal column, but no backbone. You would have to start all over from the beginning. No one could do that. It was the only justice there was. If word got out, discipline was at an end. Then soon everyone would be coming along and calling her Inge. Thirty years of professional experience thrown away. Thirty and a half, to be precise.

She pushed the overhead projector in front of the teacher's desk and set the transparent sheet down on the glass. The light was too faint, the daylight too bright. Close the curtain slightly. The lens enlarged not only the drawing, but also the chalk-dust that had gathered on the projector. Always having to dust it. Now everything was clearly recognisable: six black and white drawings of deer-like creatures eating the leaves from the trees. Big, angular, rust-brown patches, long neck. And in each drawing it became longer.

Two short-necked animals in the savannah grassland, stretching down, before they could become proper giraffes.

'As you know, giraffes live in the interior of Africa, in the savannahs, where there are short rainy seasons and long periods of drought. Then the ground becomes dry and barren. And only trees with deep roots still bear leaves. They are often the only food for giraffes. With their necks outstretched, the animals reach a height of about six metres. Their front legs are longer than their back legs, the neck is strongly elongated, the head long and the tongue very long. They are highly specialised, their whole body structure, everything looks as if it's been made specially to graze leaves from tall branches. But how the giraffe—'

A knock. Probably somewhere outside.

'. . . but how the giraffe got its long neck was given very different . . .'

Again. It was at the door. What?

'Come in!' Loud and powerful.

The door flew open. It was Kattner. The way he was standing there. Almost solemn. His ashen face. He came in, stopped, nodded to the class. In an instant they were all sitting bolt upright.

'Excuse me, Frau Lohmark.'

He always addressed her formally in front of the pupils. Concerned expression. What did he want? Did he know something?

'I'm reluctant . . .' Clearing throat. Hand in front of mouth. '. . . to disturb your lesson, but . . .'

This was it.

'Yes?'

Get in first. Not in front of the class. Don't bat an eyelid. This was her territory. The hum of the overhead projector. Very calm. Hands on the edge of the table. The frayed edges of the teacher's desk.

'. . . could you please come with me?'

Let go.

'Of course.'

But she had to take her bag. Nothing was certain. Just go after him. Upright posture. Head high. Not an eyelid. Nothing certain. Kattner waiting. Head lowered. Probably wanted to let her go first. As if he were leading her away. Which he was. How could he know anything? The clasp of her bag snapped shut. Straighten the transparency with the giraffes again. To the door.

Whispering. Anyone who whispers is lying.

'Work in silence. I'll be back directly.'

It wouldn't take long. Perhaps it would. Over and out. See you never. Door shut.

'What is it?'

'Wait a minute.'

On the wall the jellyfish and the sea anemones. She walked down the stairs behind him. His steps quick, as if he couldn't wait. Opening the door without looking at her. It wasn't especially warm. She should have put her coat on. The air, fresh and cool. Very cold on her neck. Kattner off and away. Not fully stretched since they banned him from giving speeches. Complaints at parents' evening and then the directive from the head of the school board.

Unauthorised curtailment of breaktime. Something must have happened. A teacher had been suspended at the middle school last year. Second World War marching songs in music lessons. Boozy gatherings. Unlikely that they were adults only. The bald patch on his head. Hair curling at the back of his neck. A phone-call, perhaps? From overseas. It was midnight there now. Ransom money. Traces in the woods.

Kattner's hand on the door handle. His severe expression. Still grave-looking. He opened the door. There sat Ellen. On the chair by his desk. Her arms dangling. Her hair unruly. Her angular face. Swollen eyes. She'd completely forgotten about her. A little pile of misery.

Kattner took off his jacket and hung it in the wardrobe. Hands at his side. Speech posture.

'Have you heard of something called in loco parentis?'

He put his hands on his knees and leaned down to her.

'Ellen, tell me what they did to you.'

As if on command, she started to cry.

He straightened up. Sighed.

'It's all right. Wait outside. You don't have to go back to class today.'

She dragged herself outside. Green streaks on her anorak.

He pushed the door shut behind her and shook his head.

'The girl's completely distraught.' He pulled the curtain aside and tipped the window open. Turned around. Took a deep breath.

'Tell me, do you really understand what's going on in

your class? For weeks, maybe months, that pupil has been systematically bullied, even abused.'

He sat down. He was properly angry. 'They found her in the boys' toilet. In a state that you can't imagine.' The black city moat behind the delicate leaves. The façades of the houses on the Ring yellow in the sunlight. Probably about to be torn down.

Kattner stood back up. Came closer.

'And what about you?' Folded his arms. 'Have you nothing at all to say on the matter?'

Even now they were persuading old women to pull together so that at least one house could be preserved. Forced socialisation. Probably still better than an old people's home.

'How long has it been going on like this?'

'What?'

Now he was really furious.

'A girl in your class is tortured and tormented by her fellow pupils for weeks, perhaps even months, and you claim you never noticed?'

You could still tell that you were in the East. We would see what it was like in another fifty years. Establishing a relationship took twice as long as it had lasted.

'Are you even listening?'

Yes, she was listening. She heard every single word. Not a disaster, not even the impact of a small meteorite. Just decay. It always hit someone. Group dynamics. She heard every word.

'The climate in your classroom is completely poisonous. I should have known you weren't the right one for the job.

It was all in the report. Chalk-heavy lessons. Lack of social competence. Ossified personality. But I thought, the old ones are the toughest, I even argued that you should stay here right to the end. But this is where the fun stops. This is going to have consequences.'

The aerial shot on the wall. Two letters made out of buildings in the green. The winding moat, an umbilical cord. No access to the sea. Stagnant water stinks. It was too late to split up with Wolfgang.

'You may go now.'

The corridor outside still deserted. Every lesson an eternity. Those endless forty-five minutes. The staffing plan for the next week. Bernburg's breakdown. Even suicidal thoughts supposedly. Off sick until further notice. Again. All just boxes. Consequences. There's a correct way of doing everything. That's how we do it here. And this was here now. An orderly way of doing everything. Very calm. The calm before the storm. After the storm. Her footsteps, very loud. What did regulations matter? End of the line. None of her business. Where did she come into it? Not at all. Everyone was responsible for himself. Children's voices somewhere. Of course she was to blame. So where to? Back. To class. Keep going. Service and regulation. What other chance was she left with? She was left with nothing. Everything would vanish. Sooner or later. In most cases suddenly. Like now.

Outside the rocket on the wall. High outside. The sky, still unbearably blue. Thick, white clouds. On the street side the lilacs that would soon blossom. Dried-up snowberries. Ellen on a bench. Cigarette butts in the pavement cracks. The classroom block. The painted windows of the art room.

After three steps, already breathless. Where was her stamina? The jellyfish, as shimmering and as extraterrestrially beautiful as ever. The sound of the flushing toilet. Kevin's voice. Loud laughter. Sudden silence again when she entered the biology room.

There they were once more. Beside the board. The two herds of giraffes walking towards one another. Long necks versus short necks. Which one would win? Become a giraffe, a wonder beast? A head, two metres above the heart. It must have been very strong to be able to pump blood by the litre to the brain. Only seven bones, but metres in length. The tallest of all terrestrial mammals. The right strategy. Everything had its effects, its consequences. Another five minutes till break. Another five minutes till break. Still class time. So fine.

'As you see, the ancestors of the giraffes needed a longer neck to reach the tall leaves of the trees. They must have looked more like antelopes or deer. So imagine these animals standing under the acacia trees in times of drought, and stretching themselves. Perhaps they're so hungry they even rear up, try to jump in the air. Of course it's clear that the ones among them naturally endowed with a slightly longer neck have greater chances of survival. Precisely because they can get to the food that no one else can challenge them for. So it's perfectly simple: the one with the longest neck lives longer. And the longer you survive, the greater your likelihood of procreating. And of course many animals – even the ones whose necks aren't as long – will try to reach those leaves. They will try again and again every day. Animals struggling to reach a goal that is right in front of their noses. They will train every day and develop the habit of stretching for the leaves. And slowly but surely that habit will become a way of life. And eventually it will pay off. For their children and grandchildren. The neck lengthens. Slowly but surely. Bit by bit. And generation after generation they pass on that tireless effort to their off-spring, who will in turn make a similar effort. And so one thing leads to the other. And the giraffe ends up with its long neck. And all the ones who didn't try hard enough are left with short necks and perish wretchedly. Our environment forces us all to make an effort. We all try to reach the inaccessible leaves, all the high fruits. You have to have a goal in front of you. After that, training is everything. The giraffe got its long neck because it was constantly stretching towards ever higher leaves and, as a result of that stubborn effort, that unstinting habit, its neck gradually stretched, just as we acquire muscles when we practise a sport. Life is all about stretching. For every single individual among us. Life sometimes seems within reach. But we have to make an effort actually to get there. Within each one of us there lies an urge to attain something higher, higher development. And if one places particular demands on particular parts of the body, particular organs, then they will be *encouraged* by constant, persistent challenge! Their formation is guided in a very particular direction. The desirable one, of course. Because training is the alpha and omega! The external influences have their consequences. It all has its effect on the character, on inclinations, action and body structure, on everything. And everything leads to something. Everything goes somewhere. Everything has a purpose. Whether it's living or dying. And all that effort cannot be in vain. Energy doesn't get lost! Of course we are influenced by our environment. Adaptation is everything. And habit shapes man. And if the environment changes, the organisms that live in it also change. There are no organisms without an environment.'

The bell rang.

But she wasn't finished yet.

'So of course when the giraffe's ancestors tirelessly stretched towards the leaves of the acacia trees, that had an effect too. Over many generations and long periods of time, they developed those incredibly long necks. Just as the ancestors of human beings repeatedly rose above the savannah grass to look out for enemies or prey, until at last they stood upright. Every generation inherits the fruits of the one before. Everything stacks up on top of everything else. And it's only if we strive that we achieve anything. But if we remain lazy, we lose the abilities we once acquired. Then we lose everything we've made our own. Then everything was in vain. Our muscles slacken, our ability to think declines. So we have to keep training; on no account can we stop making an effort, struggling, learning and repeating what we have learned. If everyone is always receiving support from somewhere, no one is required to look after himself. Each individual one of us has to stretch. Anything's possible as long as we really make an effort.'

What was she actually saying there? She had to sit down. Completely exhausted.

'No homework. You can go.'

Wiped out.

'Okay, let's go for it!' Girls in a row. Eyes straight ahead. Blinking. The sun.

'Today we're going to play dodgeball – to improve our stamina. Please form two groups.'

Dizzy. She had to sit down again. A bench within reach. Stretch her legs. That was better. The girls chose. Popularity before athleticism. Throw-in. The game began.

Life was aimless and random, but obligatory. In theory, anything was possible. In practice, nothing. You made a life for yourself. And after that every day was the same. Complying with circumstances. Circumstances permitting. Going on till something changed. And if something really changed, that was wrong too. Then everything went far too quickly. No telling in retrospect whether one system was worse than the other. One had proved to be more suitable. Nature didn't work in leaps. History did. If you stared at the same spot for long enough, you felt ill. Each event could be told only as a story. Just individual steps adding up. Because it was only from a series, only in sequence, one after the other, one out of the other, it was only in that way that natural history could be told. Primates were visually oriented mammals. They were eye-people. From amoeba to ape. From mosquito to elephant. A chain of being, the rise of humanity. A sequence of events, just stages, a life of imperfection, a life of not-yet. What was success in evolution? The cards were always being reshuffled. Whoever had the right one was the victor.

The girls took up their position. The ball flew. Limply. Small wonder no one was eliminated. The way they took to their heels. Forced their way to the edge of the playing field. Throwing, there was a technique to that. The goal firmly in your sights. Ideally the belly. Fat ones first. Too many targets. Get them with one shot. And out they go.

You always had to decide: attack, flee or persevere. Purely instinctive behaviour was the model for success. You had to reacquire your natural instincts. Smell the way you did billions of years ago. Walk on all fours again. A throwback, which would once again prove to be an advantage on a higher level. Later gains that more or less made up for all the losses. One step back, two steps forwards. Like something stuck. Movement, the main thing. Back to the future. There were also attempts to breed back the aurochs. At least an ox that was similar to it. With a powerful bull neck and broad horns. And with the characteristics, the properties. Conduct in nature. You would have to take all the animals that were sitting out their lives in enclosures and let them run wild. Fallow deer, moufflon, bison, wild horse, brown bear, wolf. And man? An animal that had domesticated itself. No biological necessity, a product of chance. Who said development was necessarily a good thing? Development was development. That was all. But nothing could be said without a catenation, nothing thought without valuation. Good, better, best. Even perfect eyes could waste away. Degeneration was another adaptation strategy.

The little casings of the sticky chestnut buds on the damp sand. A plastic bag chased across the playground by the wind. The first of them were gathering on the outer edge and cheering on their team. The game wasn't yet decided. Everything was still open.

Each end was an open end. Development came from unfurling. A hidden object unwrapped. From the simple to the complex. Like the core curriculum. Coming perfection, lasting adaptation. All organisms seemed to strive towards a goal. Every primordial fish, every primordial butterfly, every primordial reptile basically wanted to become a mammal. And every immaculate creature of the future. It was competition alone that impelled us onwards. And the innate propensity to progress. It was an uphill struggle. Higher, faster, further. The giraffe's neck. Water up to your neck. The cherries on the top branches, the glaciers of Greenland. They didn't need us.

Most laws were known, the forests had been cleared, the plants bred, the animals tamed. One big open-air museum. But how orderly everything was. Everything in its place. Organic and inorganic material in various aggregate states. And what did chance mean? You couldn't even imagine chance. Because of the goal. Nothing was goal-oriented. But death was the end. Provisionally. Significance was imputed everywhere. Everything that came before was a condition for all that came after. What would come after humans? There was no going back. If Is wasn't the same as Supposed-to-be, then what was it?

The eliminated players waited for the new arrivals on the

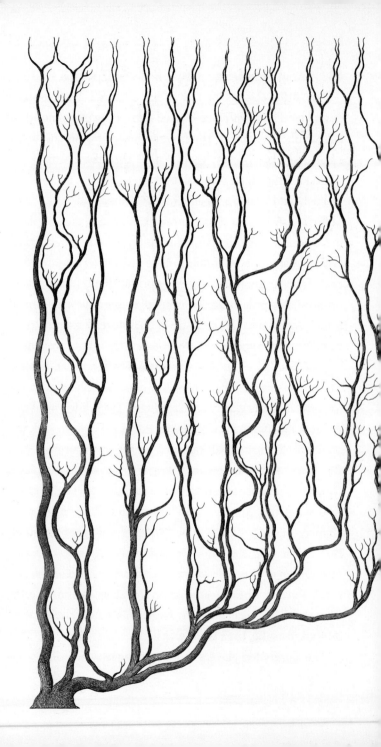

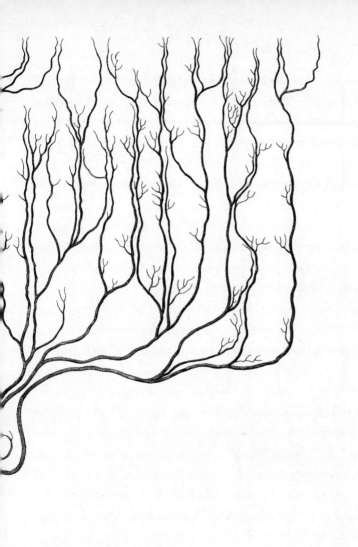

sidelines. Out of the firing line, but still there. Three-all. The girls laughed. The ball just missing one of them. Her dodge manoeuvres were bizarre. The way she stretched. Crouched. Supported herself on her hand. Toppling backwards. Now she actually fell. One of the others helped her up. On it went. The ball, harder now. It slapped a thigh. Straight hit. Out.

The winners were the most capable ones, of course. Whoever won was the rightful winner. There was no injustice in nature. No unfairness. Everything was nature. In the nature of things. If you survive, you've won. No, in fact, you haven't. If you survive, you've survived. Full stop. Today's exception could be tomorrow's rule. The only sure thing was that nothing would stay as it was. A permanent change. Inexorable. Irrevocable. It was a dynamic planet. Perfection might be striven for, but not planned for. There was no such thing as progress. Progress was an intellectual error. Everything was imperfect, but not hopeless. The present was only a transitional stage, mankind a stopgap. Every event an interim result. Everything was provisional. As Hans was always saying: the weather's right in the end, not the prognosis. Complex species had never survived for long.

It was still exciting. A wiry little thing leapt over the playing field. Like a wild animal. Her white teeth. The fresh air. How good it smelled.

The moment when swimming, when she asked herself that question for the first time. On the kitchen table in the oval zinc tub. The hot water from the big cooking pot off the stove, warm from the stovepipe, cold from the tap. Scrubbed down by her mother. The hard flannel behind her ear, between her teeth. In the green bathwater the wooden boat, an Indian canoe that her father had brought back from an official trip. What else was there but here? How old would she have been? Still in kindergarten. But already too big for the zinc tub. Her legs hung out, her feet in the dry. Always that question. Eyes on the ceiling, in the light. The lamp, a glowing milk-glass sphere at the end of a long pole. No answer. Not even the beginning of one. Nothing. Thoughts idling. She simply couldn't imagine it. And thinking: I'm sure I'll learn that in school.

Switching sides now. Back to Go. Red cheeks. Out of breath. Some even sweating. Everyone back on the playing field. Shared joy. Once more from the top.

Claudia had been mostly alone. She hadn't had any friends. Although she'd always tried. Her marks were good. Her report. In the first or second year: Claudia finds it hard to assert her positive views within the class collective. In plain words: she wasn't popular.

Sometimes she came home tear-stained. It meant they'd done something to her again. Broken her pencil, torn holes in her jumper, so big that they couldn't be darned, stolen her pen, the one that wrote in all different colours. But she never defended herself.

Not even that Friday, in the second last lesson. No one was concentrating. The class began. Claudia's seat was empty. In the third row. Far away from the teacher's desk, far away from her. Eventually she arrived. The door open just a crack and in darted Claudia. She looked distressed. Her hair over her face, puffy from weeping. She ignored their eyes and dragged herself to her seat. And then some-thing happened. She herself was standing with her back to the class, writing something on the board, when Claudia suddenly screamed. Bloodcurdling. Incredibly loud. Claudia's desk was a shambles. Her biology book was on the floor. Claudia got up. Walked forward. Straight towards her. Her shoulders were hunched, her head lowered. She whimpered: Mama. Her outstretched arms. And she? What do you want from me? Those were her words. A shove. Away from her. What did she want from her? Claudia fell. Lay there. Still crying. Lying there on the floor. Bent double. In the aisle, between the desks and chairs. In the middle of the class. Her body twitching. She could hardly breathe. Choking on her tears. Eyes closed, lips pressed together. She wouldn't stop whimpering. Mama. Over and over: Mama. A little child. Claudia was crying for her. In front of the whole class. Of course she was her mother. But first and foremost she was her teacher. She just lay there and wouldn't be calmed. No one went to her. No one comforted her. She didn't either. Out of the question. In front of the whole class. Impossible. They were in school. It was a lesson. She was Frau Lohmark.

A gust of wind. The swaying branches. Her legs felt numb. Switching ends again. Some were already wearing short trousers. Their bare, childish knees. Undamaged. The convex disc under the skin. Bare calves. Feet in trainers. Traces in the sand. Tensed muscles. Outstretched arms. The ball flew high, far too far. Far away. A short sprint. Back in play. They never tired. A ball, too hard. The girl eliminated walked sadly from the pitch. Hugged a girl behind the line. Shared sorrow. Their eyes following the ball.

From the rampart side a group of people trotting across the playground. Bent posture. In twos. A little procession towards the main building. Pensioners on the way to their course. On Fridays they start at lunchtime.

She clapped her hands.

'Very nice. That's it for today.'

They rested their hands on their knees. Gasped for breath. Took up position again.

'Until next week.' Until some time or other.

No sign of Wolfgang. He was probably in the fledglings' shed. Or over by the incubator. The sun had disappeared behind a cloud. On the left, the enclosure of the breeding threesomes. A cock stepped from the stall, strode across the meadow. A greyish-brown hen coming after him, at a suitable distance. Both leisurely, a bit wobbly, as if they were wearing high-heeled shoes. Two running lampshades. They stretched their necks slightly back and forth as they walked, always moving, seeking balance. Like a puppet. Pulled on invisible threads. Every impulse of the body was anticipated by that neck.

Two desert birds, eyeing everything and staring blankly into the distance. Creatures of the Steppes. That made sense. All of this was nothing but Steppe. It wasn't only the giraffe and the ostrich that came from Africa, man did too. But these ostriches were born here, they'd never seen their home. She'd never been to Africa either, for that matter.

Recently in Demmin they'd even set up a sturgeon breeding plant for producing caviare. Straight to the Russian market. Still: twenty jobs. Every little helps. And somewhere in Brandenburg a little herd of water buffalo was grazing in boggy wetlands. Migrant workers, all of them. The potato was an import too, of course.

Ostriches could feed even in the most barren of regions. The climate suited them. It was only in the winter that things got hard. Then it was too cold to keep the animals outside. And they refused to be locked in. For one or two days, perhaps. But after three days they were desperate to break out. They couldn't stand it. They were running birds, after all.

The other hen bent her legs and crouched down on her reptile feet under the board partition. Lying on her chest, she started giving herself a sand bath. She twisted her neck on the ground like a snake and scraped the dusty grains against her body with her short wings. The other two were now wandering along the fence that Wolfgang had rounded at the corners. The cock came closer. He stuck his head through the mesh. It was wide enough for his little skull to poke through. All birds tried to find holes to hide in, and even lower animals were skilled at judging the strength and size of their own bodies. But not ostriches. They tried to force their heads through gaps in the wire and cracks in the wood. The hiding instinct. You always had to approach ostriches with humility. Their gnarly toes in the brown mud. The thighs with their long, white bristles, fat pores, goose-bumps. The fuzzy, white petticoat under the black, yielding plumage.

Short, useless wings. Its movements, from one tuft of grass to the next, jerky and lithe, always irresolute, always oscillating between curiosity and suspicion. Its hairy nostrils. The fluff on the tiny head. The eyes were really beautiful. Two spherical apples in the tiny skull. Big, black, gleaming. The long, dark lashes. The gaze, attentive and vacuous.

Somewhere the squeak of a wheelbarrow. The ostrich immediately drew its head back. Stretched its neck. The white tail feathers went into the alarm position, the threatening posture. It charged off like that, rocking skittishly across the muddy meadow.

Now a loud rattle from the opposite stall. The door opened, and a herd of fledglings stormed out, jostling, at a gallop, taking long strides. Necks like pendulums. One animal spread its wings, and all the others did the same. The whole pack spread their wings. They ran back and forth in ever-smaller circles, beating their stumpy wings as if trying to take off. A pirouetting dance.

Loud cawing. A flock of crows apparently falling from the sky. Light as if in a film, full beam, as if everything was floodlit. The cloud, solidly outlined. Unbearable, but beautiful. The smell of soil. The ostriches danced over the meadow. Inge Lohmark stood by the fence and watched.

A NOTE ON THE TYPE

The text of this book is set in Miller. Based on the 'Scotch Roman' style, it originated in Scottish type foundries in the early nineteenth century. The version used here was designed by Matthew Carter and released by Monotype in 1997. Miller is faithful to the general characteristics of the Scotch style, though not to any particular cut, and is authentic in that it has both roman and italic small caps, a feature of the originals.